The heaviness in his chest shifted again, gathering tighter.

Isla was teasing him, laughter in her blue eyes as she relaxed in the seat next to him, and she was just so...beautiful.

Orion almost couldn't look at her, the urge to grab her and pull her into his arms nearly overwhelming him. In fact, it shocked him how tenuous his control was. If he wasn't careful, the moment they landed, he really would grab her. He'd take her upstairs and rip her clothes off before she'd even have a chance to take a breath.

But he'd already decided he wasn't going to do that, and not just with a kiss either. When they slept together again, it would be because she wanted him, because she'd asked for it, because she'd given herself to him. It wouldn't be because he'd taken it.

Jackie Ashenden writes dark, emotional stories with alpha heroes who've just gotten the world to their liking only to have it blown apart by their kick-ass heroines. She lives in Auckland, New Zealand, with her husband, the inimitable Dr. Jax, two kids and two rats. When she's not torturing alpha males and their gutsy heroines, she can be found drinking chocolate martinis, reading anything she can lay her hands on, wasting time on social media or being forced to go mountain biking with her husband. To keep up-to-date with Jackie's new releases and other news, sign up to her newsletter at jackieashenden.com.

Books by Jackie Ashenden

Harlequin Presents

The Innocent's One-Night Proposal
The Maid the Greek Married

Rival Billionaire Tycoons

A Diamond for My Forbidden Bride
Stolen for My Spanish Scandal

Three Ruthless Kings

Wed for Their Royal Heir
Her Vow to Be His Desert Queen
Pregnant with Her Royal Boss's Baby

Visit the Author Profile page
at Harlequin.com for more titles.

Jackie Ashenden

HIS INNOCENT
UNWRAPPED IN ICELAND

HARLEQUIN
PRESENTS

HARLEQUIN®
PRESENTS™

Recycling programs
for this product may
not exist in your area.

ISBN-13: 978-1-335-59308-5

His Innocent Unwrapped in Iceland

Harlequin Enterprises ULC
22 Adelaide St. West, 41st Floor
Toronto, Ontario M5H 4E3, Canada
www.Harlequin.com

Printed in U.S.A.

HIS INNOCENT
UNWRAPPED IN ICELAND

One day I'll write a book with gunfights and car chases. But it is not this day and it is not this book. :)

CHAPTER ONE

ISLA KENDRICK, DRAPED in the delicate ivory silk of her wedding gown, stood in the narthex of the ancient abbey where she was about to get married and clutched at her bouquet of delicate pink peonies as if they were a lifeline.

Orion North, the man who for the past year had been angling to take over Kendricks' Family Christmas, the company that had been in David Kendrick's family for generations and provided much of the Christmas-themed products and services around the world, surveyed her dispassionately, his amber gaze cold as it always was.

He'd simply appeared in the narthex as if by magic, and she didn't know what he was doing here. She certainly hadn't invited him to the wedding, and her adoptive father wouldn't have either. She'd met him across the boardroom table, of course, during his negotiations to buy Kendricks' off her father, and also at a few business functions she'd attended. She'd found him cold and distinctly unlikeable.

She liked him even less now.

Her two bridesmaids—her father's two secretaries, since she didn't have any sisters—were fussing with her train, but as soon as Orion had stepped into the narthex they'd stopped and stared at him instead. Unsurprisingly.

He was a man who commanded if not demanded attention, and that was only one of the reasons Isla found him so irritating.

He was six-five and broad-shouldered, built like a warrior rather than the multibillion-dollar businessman he actually was, and he towered over most people like an ancient oak towers over just about every tree in the forest. Then again, he was one of the world's most feared corporate raiders and had the cold, acquisitive gaze to match, so maybe the warrior simile was more apt.

He was also devastatingly attractive, which didn't make her any more well disposed towards him. Taken by themselves, his features were too rough and blunt for handsomeness, but there was something about their arrangement, something to do with the straight black brows and the proud jut of his nose, the curve of his lower lip, and the fact that his eyes were the colour of ancient amber that made people turn and stare.

Isla didn't want to stare. She didn't want her breath to catch every time he entered a room she was in. He was a wolf, a stone-cold predator, and she hated how he made her feel like prey. Not that he'd ever made any move towards her. Sometimes she noticed him staring at her disconcertingly from across the boardroom table, but he never said anything to her, so why he was even here she had no idea.

Just as she had no idea why he'd been circling Kendricks' for so long, not unlike a vulture circling a lion that wasn't quite dead. He hadn't made a move, though, which had made her father jumpy since North had a reputation for a quick kill when it came to acquiring companies.

He glanced at her bridesmaids and nodded towards the doors that led into the church proper. The unspoken command was clear, so they stopped fussing with Isla's train and went, leaving Isla alone with him.

A shiver of trepidation went through her, a cold feeling settling in her gut.

She'd been full of nerves this morning, wondering if she was doing the right thing in marrying Gianni, one of her father's protégés. Her father had introduced them six months earlier and Isla had known immediately that this was the sign that David thought it was time for her to settle down. Family was important for Kendricks' and most especially for the Kendricks' board. It wouldn't do for the heir to remain single, and since Gianni had been nice enough and was clearly on her father's list of approved suitors, she'd started seeing him.

And when he'd proposed six months later, she'd said yes.

She didn't love him, but that didn't matter. David thought he'd make a good husband and son-in-law and since Isla wanted to do David proud, she'd agreed. She wanted a family of her own, so why not? Except her prewedding jitters hadn't agreed, and now Orion's sudden appearance hadn't helped.

Today, he wore an expertly tailored dove-grey morning suit that made him look even more devastatingly attractive than he already was and that unsettled her even further. She was about to get married. She shouldn't be looking at other men. She shouldn't even be aware of them.

Ignoring the slow creep of ice in her gut, Isla lifted her chin and stared at the man who'd so casually interrupted the proceedings. 'What on earth are you doing here, Mr North?' She consciously tried to imitate the note of cool command her father used in the boardroom. Cool didn't come naturally to her, but she was trying. 'I'm about to get married in case you hadn't noticed and I don't believe you were invited.'

Orion's harshly carved features betrayed nothing, though there was a strange gleam in his wolf-gold eyes. 'No,' he said calmly. 'I was not.'

'Then why are you here?'

'I hate to be the bearer of bad news, Isla. But your groom isn't coming.'

The words didn't make any sense. 'Not coming?' she repeated blankly. 'What do you mean he's not coming?'

'I mean, he took a private jet out of Stansted early

this morning, bound for Rome.' Orion's cold voice was full of harsh edges and deep chasms. 'I advised him not to poach on my territory and offered him a significant amount of money to go away. So he did.'

Isla blinked. His territory? Poaching? What on earth was he talking about? 'Excuse me? You did what?'

Orion didn't move, but that odd, hot light in his eyes glinted again. 'He will not be marrying you, Isla. Not today, not tomorrow and not next week. In fact, I would go so far as to say that he will not be marrying you at all.'

A deafening silence fell in the narthex and yet Isla was conscious of a roaring in her ears. The bouquet of peonies slipped from her nerveless fingers to land in a shower of petals on the stone floor. 'What?' Her voice came out scratchy, a raw scrape of sound. 'I don't understand.'

Orion calmly bent and retrieved her bouquet from the floor just as some footsteps echoed on the stone and a man she didn't recognise came through the front door of the church. Orion murmured a few words to him and the man left again, this time going through into the church proper and closing the doors behind him.

Something was happening. Something wasn't right.

'Mr North,' she said, forcing away the cold clutch of shock. 'I want an explanation. Where is Gianni?

Why isn't he here? And what do you mean you paid him to go away?'

A rustling sound was coming from the church and the low buzz of shocked conversation. There were five hundred people out there waiting to see her get married, the cream of London high society, as well as many of her father's business cronies, not to mention Gianni's family. But something was happening there too, because they'd been silent before and they weren't now.

Orion took a step towards her and held the bouquet out to her. 'I just told you why he isn't here. He's on his way to Rome. And I paid him to go away because he should never have asked you to marry him in the first place.'

Shock was creeping through her and she had to fight to force it down. She didn't know what was happening, but going to pieces wouldn't help. Her father had always said that staying calm in a crisis was a valuable skill and one she needed to learn before she took over Kendricks' as CEO. In fact, there were many skills she needed to learn before she took over, and while some of them had been easy, others were more difficult. She had to detach, David had told her. She was too much at the mercy of her emotions.

Isla already knew that—there was a reason her first adoption had fallen through—and so when David had adopted her at twelve, she'd resolved to make sure her temper stayed leashed and she'd be the perfect daughter.

Except keeping her emotions locked down with shock coursing through her veins and a man she didn't like standing in front of her telling her that he'd paid her fiancé to jilt her, her brittle, cool authority was in danger of cracking entirely.

'Why on earth shouldn't he have asked me to marry him?' she demanded.

'Because he doesn't love you,' Orion said without hesitation. 'And you don't love him.'

Isla stared at him in astonishment. This made no sense, none of it. His presence, Gianni's absence, what he was saying to her...

'That...' she said stupidly. 'That's none of your business.'

'It's true, though.' There was a note of certainty in his voice. As if he knew her feelings better than she did herself. 'You're marrying him because David wanted you to.'

Anger stirred inside her, threatening her grip on her detachment. 'Don't be ridiculous. You know nothing about me or Gianni.' She snatched her bouquet from him and straightened, trying to inject some steel into her spine, projecting 'future CEO' and not 'angry orphan'. 'I don't care what you paid him or why. You need to bring him back this instant.'

Orion simply looked at her, the glitter of the wolf in his eyes. 'No,' he said in the same calm tone. 'I will not.'

Her fingers felt cold, and she could hear the buzz

of conversation from the assembled guests. It was louder now.

It couldn't be true. It couldn't be happening. Surely Gianni was already at the altar, waiting for her. Surely he was.

He would have sent someone to see what the delay was about by now.

True. Yet no one had come except that employee of Orion's.

Ice crept through her as reality began to assert itself. Gianni didn't appear and neither did her father, and all she could hear was the conversation of the guests, getting even louder.

While Orion merely stood there looking at her, dressed in his exquisite grey morning suit.

The roaring was back in her ears, the floor feeling as if it had shifted beneath her feet and then unexpectedly, a large, warm hand was beneath her elbow.

Orion. His grip was firm and strong, the solidity of mountains keeping her upright, and for a split second, she almost leaned into his hold, because her knees felt weak.

'I know this is a shock,' he continued in that same steady, implacable tone. 'But I'm not here to hurt you.'

'I don't understand.' She hated how uncertain and weak she sounded. 'Why are you here then?'

His palm beneath her elbow was warm, in stark contrast to the cool of his voice. Yet his amber eyes gleamed with a sudden, dark fire. 'Why do you think? I'm here to marry you instead, Isla.'

Orion watched Isla's pretty blue eyes widen in shock.

He wasn't surprised. It was, after all, a very shocking proposal.

Yet that had been the plan he'd been formulating for the past month, ever since he'd found out that Isla Kendrick was going to marry one of her father's protégés. Orion simply couldn't allow that to happen.

He'd been playing the long game for months now, deciding initially that he'd take the slow, careful approach with her. Then her engagement had been announced, which he hadn't been expecting, and he'd had to rethink his plans.

He wasn't in love with her—love wasn't possible for him these days—but he'd admit to being in the grip of a singular…fascination with her.

It had all started at a business gala held at the National Gallery, where he'd found her standing in a small gallery away from the crowd, in front of a painting, and there had been a rapt look on her face.

He hadn't known who she was, but she'd seemed illuminated, lit from within by something he didn't understand and his interest had been caught. He'd checked the painting to see what it was that held her attention so completely. But it was only Van Gogh's painting of a night sky.

Orion didn't like it when he didn't understand something. His instinct was always to make sense of it, so he'd gone over and asked her what was so interesting about the painting.

She'd smiled, like the sun rising on a midwinter morning, and started talking about the brushstrokes, the layers of the paint, the flowing motion of the painted sky and how they came together to form a beautiful, luminous whole. Her hands had moved as she spoke, as eloquent and graceful as her words, and he'd been…transfixed.

He'd never much appreciated art and the creative impulse was a mystery to him. He was a man who took things apart. He didn't create. He'd tried once, long ago, to build something, but that had left him broken, so now he didn't bother. Satisfaction came from looking at a system that wasn't performing, at identifying why it wasn't and what was broken, and then deciding what to do about it. Rather like a mechanic taking apart an old car and selling some parts for scrap, while reconditioning other parts to make it go better.

He was good at it.

So it was all very mysterious why he'd found looking at this woman while she talked about a bit of paint on a board so fascinating. There was something about her. About the way she came alive that consumed his interest so completely he hadn't been able to do anything but stare.

That was the night he'd decided that he simply had to know more about her.

It hadn't taken him long to discover that she was

David Kendrick's adopted daughter, Isla, the apparent heir to Kendrick's underperforming Christmas company. Her adoption thirteen years earlier, at the age of twelve, had been a media sensation—'Childless Christmas company magnate adopts orphan girl at Christmas time!'—and Kendrick had made much of her potential. Having been an orphan himself, Orion was further intrigued to see what kind of businesswoman she'd grown into. Perhaps she came alive when talking about sales projections as well as paintings?

However, that turned out to be not the case which at first he'd found underwhelming. She was quiet, barely saying a word even when asked, and she seemed uncertain of herself. Not at all the hungry go-getter Kendrick had always portrayed her to be and not at all that luminous woman he'd seen in the gallery that night.

Her milkmaid appearance didn't help the CEO image, all spun gold hair, dark blue eyes and peaches and cream complexion. She looked like a porcelain doll—if a porcelain doll had been petite and curvy, all rounded breasts, hips and thighs. The male animal in him had appreciated the feminine in her, and while he certainly found her lovely, she didn't have the same luminosity in the boardroom that she had in the gallery.

It puzzled him and, since he liked a puzzle, he'd arranged more meetings with Kendrick on the pretext of buying his company, but in reality wanting to observe Isla Kendrick more closely and find out just what was so fascinating about her.

She was always very polished and put together, yet he'd noticed that sometimes a lock of blond hair would come loose from its elegant chignon. That her red lipstick was sometimes smudged a little at the side of her pouty mouth. Or that the top button of her white tailored blouses had a tendency to come undone.

And that wasn't all. There were moments in the boardroom on the rare occasions she spoke, where although she seemed poised, he was certain that she wasn't. Where he sensed she was out of her depth. It seemed so at odds with the woman who spoke so knowledgeably and confidently about the painting, that he found himself to be even more intrigued.

On a number of occasions during those meetings, he'd tried having a conversation with her, but it soon became clear that she didn't like him and avoided him. He was used to being disliked. No one warmed to the pirate who boarded their ship and took all their gold, after all, but he found it…annoying when it came to her.

He'd been planning on how to overcome her dislike when news of her engagement had broken. And that's when he'd decided she would be his next takeover.

There had only been a week between her engagement and the date for her wedding, which meant there had been no time for the 'slow and careful' approach. No time for finesse or subtlety. He'd already discovered by then that the marriage had been engineered by Kendrick himself to improve her already poor standing with the company board and hardly the love match portrayed in the press—not that he would have put his plans on hold even if she had been in love—so he had no qualms about making his move on her wedding day.

It was the perfect opportunity to use shock to his advantage in order to get what he wanted, and he wouldn't have been the ruthless businessman he was if he hadn't made the most of his opportunities. He was a man who got what he wanted, when he wanted it, and he wanted her.

He'd gone to Kendrick the night before and told him that he wanted Isla, and that if Kendrick knew what was good for his company, he'd let Orion have her. The old man though hadn't just rolled over. Orion's interest in Kendricks' had unsettled him and he'd known his company was vulnerable to a takeover. So he'd told Orion that if he wanted Isla, not only would he have to buy Kendricks' outright for an extortionate amount, but he'd have to retain Isla as CEO for the optics—a family Christmas company needed a Kendrick to remain in charge and preferably a married Kendrick. Oh, yes, and he'd also insisted that Orion keep the company intact and Isla as CEO and his wife for at least a year, before making a decision about what to do with either.

Orion had no feelings at all about the company— he'd keep it the year Kendrick specified but then he'd

likely break it up and sell the more profitable parts—
nor did he care whether Isla stayed on as CEO. But
he wanted to secure his asset and if he had to marry
her to secure her, he would. He didn't mind marrying
her. Marriage had always seemed a pointless institu-
tion to him and a year should be more than enough
time to explore his fascination with her.

Not that a year of marriage was his biggest issue
right now.

No, his biggest issue was going to be getting her
to agree to go through with it.

Luckily, he had leverage on his side in the form of
Kendricks' itself, plus a few well-rehearsed speeches
about how it would be a win-win situation for both
of them. All he had to do was convince her.

The frothing fall of her veil didn't hide how her
dark blue eyes had deepened into indigo with shock
or how white she'd gone. Almost as white as her
wedding gown.

'Marry you?' Her light, cool voice had gone
hoarse. 'Are you mad?'

'No,' he said, smiling slightly. 'Think of it as an
opportunity.'

'An opportunity?' A couple more petals from the
poor, abused peonies in her hand drifted to the stone
floor. 'An opportunity for what?'

He tightened his grip on her elbow a little, hoping the physical touch would jolt her out of her shock
response. Nothing to do with how the warmth of her
silken skin under his fingers made his breath catch.

It had been a reflexive thing to steady her, but now he was touching her, he couldn't bring himself to let her go.

'An opportunity for you to save Kendricks',' he replied. He preferred not to use threats when it came to business negotiations, but he would if it got him what he wanted. So he let her see the pirate, the ruthless part of him that had driven him from a hand-to-mouth existence as an unwanted orphan, to being CEO of one of the world's most dangerous acquisitions companies. 'I went to your father last night and we had a very interesting discussion. He was quite happy for me to marry you instead of Gianni, as long as I not only bought Kendricks', but kept you as CEO. I did make him a promise to keep the company intact for at least a year, but...' He lifted a shoulder. 'Perhaps I won't. Perhaps I'll break it up and sell it for a healthy profit. Unless of course my wife advises me otherwise.'

Anger sparked suddenly in her blue eyes and a hint of colour washed through her pale cheeks. That was good. She had a bit of backbone it seemed. 'If you expect that I'm going to let you—'

'Think,' he murmured, giving her elbow another squeeze, watching how the reminder of his touch made the colour in her cheeks deepen still further. Interesting. He was well aware that she didn't like him, but that blush indicated that she was affected by his hand on her arm at least, which was pleasing. 'As CEO and my wife, you'll be able to discuss with me any restructures. Perhaps you might advise against them. Perhaps I might listen to you.'

She took a breath and he watched as she visibly forced aside her shock, her pretty features hardening. It was impressive. Was this the potential her father had seen in her? Certainly it was more feeling than he'd ever observed in the boardroom.

'Is that a threat?'

'Not at all. As I said, I'm merely pointing out an opportunity.'

'Or you could just not buy Kendricks' at all,' she said coldly. 'Or not be my stand-in groom. You could just go back to doing what you do best which is destroying things. How's that for an opportunity?'

He allowed himself another smile. Oh, she definitely had more backbone than he'd expected, which was pleasing. However, she didn't know him. She didn't know that he never gave up when he wanted something, never ever. Once, long ago, when he'd still had a conscience and a heart that hadn't completely frozen over, he'd let something go. Something very, very precious to him. But he never would again. The conscience he'd once had was dead and so was his heart, and now nothing could touch him.

'I could,' he said. 'But alas, I wish to marry you more.'

Beyond the big doors of the church's interior, he could hear more rustlings as people shifted in their seats, the hum of conversation now a dull roar.

He needed her to make a decision and to make it quickly.

'I won't require anything of you,' he went on, keeping his voice low and steady. 'It'll be a marriage in name only. We can hash out the details on our honeymoon.'

Isla was white beneath her veil, but he could see her pretty mouth. The lipstick she had on today was a soft pink, highlighting the lush fullness of her lips. 'A honeymoon? You can't be serious.'

'Of course I'm serious.' He'd already planned it out in the hours before the wedding, because he was nothing if not prepared. 'We will need a honeymoon to let the dust settle here and so we can discuss our arrangement.' And so he could discover his own peculiar fascination with her.

She was staring at him now as if she'd never seen him before in all her life. 'So let me get this straight,' she said slowly. 'If I don't marry you today, now, you'll remove me as CEO and break Kendricks' up?'

'Correct.'

'But that's blackmail.'

He lifted a shoulder. 'I prefer to think of it as an incentive.'

'But you're not giving me a choice.'

'Naturally, you have a choice. You can choose not to marry me. I'm not forcing you into anything.'

Her gaze behind her veil was very dark, her posture stiff, and he could feel the tension in her arm.

Time was passing and they'd been standing there

too long, and if he waited any longer, her shock would wear off and she would start thinking clearly and logically, and his window of opportunity would be gone. He couldn't let that happen.

'Come,' he murmured. 'We can't stay here too much longer. People are getting impatient. You can refuse, in which case I'll leave, then take the company anyway, removing you as CEO and your father gets nothing. Or you can agree, in which case your father gets the nice little windfall from the sale of the company he was expecting, you get to remain as CEO and I get to keep the company intact for the year that I promised. You might even convince me to keep it intact longer than a year.'

She was trembling slightly. 'You're a bastard.'

Unperturbed, Orion inclined his head. He'd expected her anger. 'Indeed. Though, I've been called worse.'

'Doesn't it matter to you at all that you paid my fiancé off? That you—'

'Enough with the outrage,' he interrupted mildly. 'You didn't love him, as I already pointed out. You don't love me either, so really, all you're doing is swapping one means to an end with another. It's no big deal.'

The blush in her cheeks burned more intensely, which intrigued him. He'd assumed that her tremble was fear, and though he hadn't wanted to frighten her, he'd accepted that she might be afraid. However, that blush wasn't fear, that was anger.

Good. Anger was better than fear. It was certainly more powerful.

'No big deal?' she hissed. 'Are you mad?'

'Isla,' he murmured. 'Yes or no.'

For a second he thought she might refuse and his muscles tensed in response.

Then she tore her arm from his grip. Yet instead of heading out of the church and escaping, she marched straight over to the big oak double doors that led to the church proper. She stopped in front of them, clutching the remains of her peonies in a white-knuckled grip. 'Come on then,' she said, not looking at him. 'Let's get this over with.'

Orion smiled. She had more spirit than he'd expected, a lot more, in fact. And he liked that. He liked it very much.

So he came over to where she stood, and pushed open the doors, and let the strains of the wedding march fill the church.

CHAPTER TWO

ISLA IGNORED THE stares of the guests as she and Orion stepped through the doors. She ignored her father standing there, and the look of relief on his face.

Anger seethed in the pit of her stomach, and it was only sheer force of will that was preventing her from flinging her bouquet in Orion's stupid, smug face, kicking her father in the shins, then running straight out the doors and never coming back.

But anger wouldn't help, it never did, and she had no choice now but to hold tight to her bouquet and act as though the change of groom had been her idea all along.

Firstly she could barely believe Orion had gone to her father and done this apparent deal for her behind her back, without even a word to her. Secondly, she could barely believe her father had agreed to it.

Then again, maybe it wasn't so difficult to believe. Orion's reputation as a businessman who got what he wanted was well-known, and as for her father, Kendricks' and its legacy was the only thing that mattered to him. That's why he'd adopted her, to take over the helm once he was gone. He certainly hadn't cared who her groom was as long as it was someone. And from a business perspective selling Kendricks' made sense—the board was unhappy and the company had been underperforming for years—and extracting a promise from Orion to keep it intact had been a good move. As had making sure she stayed on as CEO in order to retain the illusion of family control.

Yet she was furious all the same that David hadn't said anything to her, leaving her to have to deal with Orion turning up just before she had to walk down the aisle.

Leaving her to deal with Orion's threats to Kendricks' if he didn't marry her.

Because of course, she couldn't allow that to happen. The whole reason she'd been adopted had been to take over Kendricks' since her father hadn't had any other children. His wife hadn't been able to have them and after she'd died, he hadn't wanted to marry again. Yet Kendricks' was a family company and because he'd wanted to pass it on to a child of his, he'd decided to adopt. And she'd been his choice.

Which also made Orion her problem to fix.

She had no idea why he wanted to marry her, none at all. Apart from that one conversation in the National Gallery where he'd rudely turned around and walked out, he'd never shown her the slightest bit of interest. So for him to turn up here, telling her that he'd paid Gianni off and that he'd take Kendricks' if she didn't marry him… It was baffling.

Regardless of his reasons, that didn't make her any less furious. Furious with him for threatening her into this and furious at herself, because surely, she should have anticipated this. Perhaps not his arrival at her wedding or his paying off Gianni, but surely she should have felt alarm bells at his interest in Kendricks' and wondered why he hadn't moved to acquire it straight away.

David had taught her to be sharp and observant in the boardroom, yet she hadn't noticed Orion betray anything more than his usual cold interest.

And you know why you didn't notice, don't you?

Isla gritted her teeth, keeping her gaze squarely on the altar at the end of the aisle and not on the shocked gazes of the guests.

Yes, she knew. She just hated to admit that the reason she hadn't noticed anything untoward about Orion was that she'd tried very hard not to notice him at all. He unsettled her, he always had, right from the first moment he'd walked into the boardroom a week after their first meeting at the National Gallery a year ago. He'd brought some kind of hissing, crackling electricity with him that had found its way under her skin, making her feel antsy and restless and bothered.

She'd hated it. Emotions had no place in the boardroom, as she well knew. She had to be cool and sharp, and she was learning to be both, but it was something she'd always found difficult. She felt things deeply and passionately, and even the years in the foster system hadn't quite put out the fire that burned in her heart. The fire that Orion's mere presence only stoked, apparently. She'd tried to tune him out whenever he was around, tried to pretend she didn't notice when his gaze rested on her, staying quiet and still in the hope that he'd lose whatever interest in her he had. Except that hadn't worked because if it had, she wouldn't be walking down the aisle with him right now.

She should have paid attention. If she'd put her personal feelings aside and talked to him, discovered what his intentions were with Kendricks' and with her, then perhaps this could have been avoided.

It doesn't help that the board don't want you at the helm.

That was also true. They were dissatisfied with her performance—they hadn't thought she was CEO material—and that made the company vulnerable to someone like Orion, a wolf lying in wait looking for prey to attack and pull apart.

It was a vulnerability she'd been hoping to fix. David had adopted her to be the future of Kendricks' and the marriage to Gianni was supposed to help cement that future with the board. Some of them wouldn't like this new development with Orion, but it was likely the majority would approve—they might even like him better than Gianni, in which case marrying him would achieve the same aim. But only if it looked like her decision rather than a deal done behind her back between Orion and her father, that she had no part in.

So you'd better keep smiling and acting like this was all your idea, hadn't you?

Isla shoved down her anger and bitter self-recriminations as she came to a stop before the altar, forcing herself to smile. There was a murmured exchange between Orion and the vicar, who then launched into the marriage service.

Dead silence fell over the entire church.

It didn't matter that it wasn't the wedding she'd thought she'd have.

It didn't matter that Orion had paid off the man she'd thought she was going to marry and Gianni had… Well, he'd taken the money and run.

You can't have been that important to him. He didn't really want to marry you. He didn't want a wife any more than David had wanted a daughter.

Something ached and burned in her heart, but she was familiar with the sensation, so she ignored it. Instead, she concentrated on saying her vows when prompted, then listening to Orion say his. And when he held out his hand, she gave it to him. He produced a ring from his pocket and slid it onto her finger, and dimly it occurred to her that there were a whole lot of questions she should be asking him. Such as why he was marrying her in the first place and how long had he been planning for it.

People were murmuring, and that was no surprise.

They'd all be wondering why the Kendricks' heir was suddenly walking down the aisle with a different man, and what had happened to her original groom.

What must they think of you? What must David think of you? He sold you to one man first, before selling you off to another...

She felt cold, the winter outside penetrating the stone of the church, or maybe it wasn't the winter. Maybe it was just the cold settling down inside her, a slow creeping shock she couldn't shake.

Yet she couldn't allow that to take hold, just as she couldn't keep going back over that late-night phone conversation of her father's that she shouldn't have overheard.

She was standing before the altar, with people staring at her, and she couldn't afford to look weak and uncertain in front of them, not when her suitability as future CEO was already being questioned. She had to look strong and in control, as if this had been her decision all along, not one forced on her.

So she put some steel into her spine as Orion took hold of her veil and lifted it. His gaze wasn't cold now. Instead, it burned with a dark golden flame that made her heart beat inexplicably fast.

She didn't like him. Everything about him made her restless and uneasy, and the way he was looking at her now...

Gianni never looked at you that way.

No, he hadn't. He'd liked her and the kisses they'd shared had been pleasant if undemanding. But he'd never looked at her the way Orion was looking at her. As if he wanted to eat her alive…

Her heartbeat thumped loudly in her head as Orion bent and brushed his mouth over hers. It was the world's most fleeting kiss and even though she'd been expecting it, she hadn't been expecting the static electricity that prickled over her skin the moment their lips met.

It was the same electricity she felt whenever he was around, the one that made her restless and unsettled, that made the fire inside her flicker and leap. Now it was as if that electricity had found its way beneath her skin, shocking her in ways she didn't expect.

You should have just walked out of the church and damn the consequences.

She should have. But it was too late now.

Orion lifted his head, tucking her hand into his elbow, and then they were walking back up the aisle, now husband and wife.

She felt icy yet her lips burned from that brief kiss. Ignoring both sensations, she kept her chin lifted and her spine straight, ignoring the shocked expressions on the faces of the wedding guests.

It was completely her choice to marry the man who'd been going to acquire Kendricks'. A shock move, yes, but as Orion had said, it was an opportunity.

An opportunity to keep Kendricks' safe and stay

in control as CEO. Perhaps also an opportunity to learn more about the enemy.

Talk it up all you want. The truth is that all of this is your fault. If you'd been able to realise the potential your father saw in you, then Orion wouldn't have targeted Kendricks' in the first place.

Isla shoved the thought away. She'd fix this. She would.

As they stepped out of the church, it was snowing. David had thought a December wedding would be perfect since the marriage of the Kendricks' heir really should take place at Christmas time, and Isla had agreed.

Except it was cold, the icy breeze whispering over her exposed skin and making her shiver.

Somehow Orion had the thick white shawl she'd bought for this moment and for the photos, and he placed it around her shoulders. 'I will be coming shortly,' he murmured and then someone else in a dark uniform was at her side, ushering her along to the icy path to the church gate.

The tight knot in her chest that had gathered in anticipation of the confrontation that would no doubt occur with her father loosened a little. Clearly there was to be no confrontation with either her guests or her father, or at least, not one that she'd have to deal with.

Still, she felt like a coward as she went through the church gate without a protest and then into the long black car that stood idling at the kerb.

It was warm inside the car, the butter-soft leather of the seats enveloping her as she was bundled inside, the train of her gown folded in neatly with her.

Then there was silence.

Had it really happened? Had she really married Orion North?

A shudder worked its way down her spine, but Isla pushed the weakness viciously away. It was done now. She'd have to deal with David at some point, not to mention the media fallout, but the main thing was that Kendricks' was safe. That was assuming Orion was a man of his word.

You should have got an assurance of that in writing before *you married him.*

Isla sat back in her seat, still feeling cold, trying to ignore the voice in her head. She hadn't thought of getting an agreement from him in the narthex. She'd been in shock and he'd taken advantage of that mercilessly. And she'd been the one to stamp angrily to the church doors, telling him to 'get this over with'.

She'd been stupid, allowed her anger at his threat to get to her, and had handled this thing badly. But there was no use beating herself up about it. She'd done it now and the only way forward was to protect Kendricks' from Orion any way she could.

'Mrs North?' The driver was holding a phone out to her from the front seat. 'Mr North would like a word.'

Isla blinked. Yes, that's right. She was Mrs North

now, wasn't she? She leaned forward and took the phone, raising it to her ear. 'Yes?'

'I'm staying to clear up matters here.' Orion's deep voice was as cool as the snow falling outside. 'Also to have a word with your father. I'll meet you at the airport.'

The airport. They were going to airport. And *he* was going to talk to her father.

'I see,' she said, ignoring the anger that had resumed boiling at the calm way he'd taken charge of everything. 'I'd appreciate it if you informed my father to be clear to the media and the board that this was *my* decision, not some shady backroom deal you two did between yourselves behind my back.'

'Of course,' Orion said smoothly and without a trace of shame. 'After all, it *was* your decision.'

Isla gritted her teeth. 'And the reception? The guests?' There, she could sound as cool and as calm as he did.

'Leave that to me. I'm sure you'd prefer to avoid any awkwardness.'

It was so close to the truth that she was very tempted to open the car door and go running back into the church just to prove him wrong. But that *would* be letting her emotions get the better of her. Perhaps it would look more powerful if she let him explain. After all, this was all his doing.

'Fine,' she said, giving him nothing.

'Good.' He sounded infuriatingly smug. 'My jet will be waiting for you to relax in.'

'Lovely.' She meant the opposite.

'We'll be taking a flight to Iceland where I have a lodge. We can spend some time there talking about where we go from here. Or would you prefer the tropics?'

She and Gianni had planned a week's honeymoon in the Caribbean. She hadn't been looking forward to it, though she hadn't been able to put her finger on why. Probably because she hadn't felt she could take a week off, nothing at all to do with the thought of spending a week in Gianni's company.

'Does it matter?' she asked, feeling suddenly exhausted.

'No,' Orion said. 'Iceland it is.' Then his voice changed, warming fractionally. 'Don't worry, Isla. I'll deal with it all.'

There shouldn't have been any reason for her to like the way he'd said that any better than the way he'd said everything else. Yet for some reason she found his casual reassurance...relieving. Because right now, yes. She wanted someone else to deal with it.

Someone who won't make a mess of everything.

'I should speak to David myself,' she said, ignoring the thought.

'Perhaps later,' Orion said casually. 'I'm talking to him right now. All you need to do is get on the plane.' Then without even saying goodbye, he ended the call.

Isla let out a breath, handed the phone back to the

driver, then leaned back in her seat as the car finally pulled away and into the snowy village road.

Her thoughts whirled, but she ignored them all, staring out at the snow falling on the villages they passed. Trying not to feel the slight pressure of her new wedding ring on her finger, or think about the million questions she wanted answers to. Because the man she wanted those answers from wasn't here.

Eventually the car pulled into a private airfield, where a sleek little jet waited on the runway. The driver helped Isla out of the car and up the stairs, and soon she was inside and ensconced in another extremely comfortable soft leather seat.

She took off her veil and folded it neatly, setting it onto the seat beside her, before drawing the shawl more firmly around her shoulders. A stewardess approached with a glass of champagne, which Isla found a little on the nose since there wasn't anything to celebrate from her perspective. But since it seemed churlish to refuse and quite frankly, she could use a drink, she took it.

A short time later, the jet's door opened in a rush of cold air, and Orion strode in.

Snow dusted the shoulders of his morning suit and his coal-black hair, but he didn't look cold or seem bothered by it in the least. In fact, judging from his expression, what he seemed was extremely pleased with himself. Not unlike an ancient Roman emperor about to embark on a triumph down the Appian Way.

Isla was almost surprised that he wasn't cloaked in purple and wearing a laurel wreath.

A good thing. It would suit him far too well.

She tried to drag her gaze away from him as he paused to talk to the stewardess, but it was difficult.

He was her husband and the electricity that had slid beneath her skin during their kiss at the altar was again humming and crackling, making her feel restless, unable to sit still.

She hadn't liked it then and she didn't like it now, most especially because she had an idea what it was: physical attraction. She'd hadn't felt it with Gianni and she'd liked him, so why she should feel it for a man who was essentially the enemy, she had no idea. It bothered her, especially when that brief kiss at the altar still burned in her memory.

Forcing her gaze from Orion's mesmerising figure, Isla stared out the window into the swirling snow as the plane taxied down the runway and lifted into the air, trying to think of absolutely nothing. But then, as they reached cruising altitude, she became aware of someone tall and powerful and very definitely male approaching and sitting in the seat opposite her.

Her heart thudded and she tensed.

'Come now, Isla,' Orion said, clearly noticing her tension. 'The hard part is over. Now you can relax.'

Bracing herself, she took her gaze from the window and looked at him.

He was sitting with his elbows on his knees, his

hands clasped between them, and his gaze fixed on her with disturbing intensity. He smiled and it was so full of an unexpected, slow-burning heat her breath caught.

He was looking at her as if she was a prize he'd fought for hard and won.

She could feel herself blushing, the electricity under her skin prickling.

Even your own father never looked at you that way, as if you were worth something.

The thought wound through her, a small thread of jagged ice. David had certainly been pleased with her when he'd first adopted her. He'd been satisfied with her excellent marks at school and the reports detailing her potential, as well as her polite manner and how articulate she was. Smart, he'd called her, and she'd been thrilled. She hadn't cared that he was the Christmas magnate and he'd adopted her to be his heir. She'd just been happy someone had wanted her, and she'd been excited to be part of a family again.

She'd thought he wanted a daughter, but it soon became apparent that David had no use for daughters, and what he actually wanted was a business protégé, an employee he could mould into his perfect successor. He found her emotional needs tiresome, frequently telling her that he hadn't adopted her because he wanted hugs and family time. He'd adopted her because her school marks were excellent and she had potential. A potential she knew she hadn't lived up to.

But she didn't want to think about that. The only thing that mattered right now was getting answers from Orion North.

Ignoring the heat in her cheeks and the electricity in her bloodstream, Isla forced herself to hold his gaze. 'So, Mr North,' she said flatly. 'You promised me Kendricks' would remain intact for a year if I married you, and that I would be CEO. So now I have, in fact, married you, I want that promise in writing and I want it now.'

Orion contemplated the new Mrs Isla North with not a little bit of satisfaction.

She looked like a snow maiden, all swathed in white, and yet there were so many delicate colours to her. Colours he'd never noticed before. The angry sapphire of her eyes and her full, pink mouth. The rose petal stain of a blush on her cheeks and the golden curls escaping from her careful bridal up-do and falling down around her ears.

His wife now.

Even though marriage had never been his intention—or at least not until a week earlier—he found the thought of her being his wife very satisfying. He'd promised Kendrick he'd stay married to her for a year, not that he cared overmuch about time frames since it probably wouldn't take all that long to get to the bottom of his fascination with her. And once he had, he'd already decided that they'd lead separate lives until the year was up and then he'd divorce her.

He had no need for a wife and a family was not on his list of things to accomplish. He had no things to accomplish, not since he'd already accomplished everything he'd set out to do. All except one, of course. But that was something that would remain undone.

However, now Isla was his, he could take some time to find out exactly what it was about her that drew him so intensely.

Certainly he'd admired her poise back in the church. She'd been furious, but she'd taken him and his threat seriously and hadn't balked when he'd promised to carry it through if she didn't agree to be his wife. And, of course, a written agreement was exactly what he'd demand if he was in her shoes.

Which was why he'd already had his legal department draw one up.

'Funny you should ask.' He lifted a hand. Obligingly, the stewardess came over with the agreement that she'd just finished printing out and handed it to him.

He took it and held it out to Isla. 'I trust this will suffice.'

The look she gave him was deeply suspicious as she reached for the papers, and became even more so when he didn't let them go.

The colour of her eyes was so very pretty. A deep, endless blue, like a summer sky at midnight. He'd liked it when he'd lifted her veil by the altar and had looked down into them, seeing all those challenging, glittering sparks.

It wasn't the same as when she'd talked to him about that Van Gogh painting and she'd become so luminous he hadn't been able to look away, yet it was similar.

You want her to come alive for you too.

Maybe he did. He certainly didn't need to hold on to the papers the way he was doing now, but he was and purely to see that hot blue flame burn in her gaze.

'I don't know if it will suffice,' she said. 'Not if you don't let me look at it.'

Really, she was quite delicious like this, all pink and white and furious. If he'd known, he'd have somehow engineered things so he could have married her sooner. Either that or he'd have seduced her. Though, he could still seduce her. He'd told her in the church it would be a marriage in name only, but that had been before he'd got close to her. Before he'd touched her silky skin and kissed that soft pouty mouth in front of the altar.

In fact, he was starting to think that perhaps he might want a wedding night, and perhaps she might agree. After all, she wasn't unaffected by him, not given the way she was blushing now.

Clearly it was time to test that.

'Say please,' he murmured.

She blinked. 'Excuse me?'

'I think you heard.' He smiled. 'Politeness is key to any business negotiation.'

More anger glittered in her eyes and he liked it.

He liked it far too much. She'd been so very contained in all those business meetings he'd had with her and her father, and yet he'd had the sense that her control was imperfect. Sometimes her fingers would drum on the desk or she'd tap her foot on the floor. Or she'd shift minutely in her seat, as if she couldn't sit still.

She seemed like a champagne bottle that had been shaken with the cork still in it, all the liquid fizzing and seething inside just waiting for a chance to explode.

Perhaps he might see that explosion now.

The thought made him catch his breath.

'Please,' she said through gritted teeth.

Disappointing. He didn't want her to give in. He wanted her to fight. He wanted her to come alive the way she had in the National Gallery, and he didn't even know why.

That he no longer experienced the passion he'd seen in her face that day perhaps accounted for it. He didn't have room in his life for feelings that intense, not any more. He allowed himself moments of physical pleasure, but beyond that, the only thing that held his interest was the pursuit of underperforming companies. The thrill of the chase.

He hadn't known he'd wanted more than that until he'd seen Isla Kendrick explain to him why *Starry Night* by Vincent Van Gogh was one of her favourite paintings and what made it so transformative.

He hadn't understood what she was talking about

when she'd explained, but he'd understood that look on her face. He wanted to see it again.

He wanted to see it for *him*.

'Oh, no,' he chided gently. 'That's no way to drive a bargain. You don't give in straight away. You negotiate. You make a counter offer.'

'This is not a negotiation, Mr North. This is you giving me some papers to look over.'

'Mr North? I'm your husband, Isla. The least you could call me is Orion.'

'I'd much prefer to call you a stone-cold bastard, how does that sound?'

He smiled. 'That's the spirit. How about this then? I'll give you the agreement to look over in return for a kiss.'

She flushed. 'Absolutely not. I don't need to read it that badly.'

'*Au contraire.* If you don't read it, then I can't sign it. And if I don't sign it, you won't get my promise in writing, and Kendricks' will still be at risk.'

Emotions flickered over her face, gone so fast he couldn't read them all. Fury seemed to be her primary emotion, and he couldn't blame her. He had, after all, completely upset her wedding day by paying off her ridiculous excuse for a fiancé, and threatening to get rid of her as CEO and take apart her company if she didn't marry him. That couldn't have been easy for her, yet she'd coped with it all admirably, displaying unexpected backbone.

She was proving to be much more interesting

than he'd anticipated and he was intrigued to see where this fury might lead her. Anger could be far more productive and useful if it was properly focused, and it was certainly preferable to her being upset or afraid.

In fact, he didn't like the thought of her being upset or afraid.

Isla gave him a look of disdain from beneath long, feathery golden lashes. 'You've already had one kiss. You don't get another.'

'Then offer me something else,' he countered. 'Something you can give me right now, that's easy and quick and something I want.'

Her blue gaze narrowed. 'What do you want then?'

Orion was a gambler and he never gave anything away. He kept his cards close to his chest, what little emotion he allowed himself under strict control and his desires very firmly hidden. Not that he had any desires. Desiring nothing meant no one had power over you, and if there was one thing he hated, it was anyone having any kind of power over him.

These days, *he* was the one with the power. He held all the cards and he won all the games. Always.

He smiled. 'Guess.'

The explosion he'd been hoping for didn't come. Instead, she let go of the papers and sat back in her seat, regarding him with a cool blue stare. 'You know, I really don't like you. In fact, I've never liked you.'

He only raised a brow. 'That has never been a barrier to people doing business with me.'

'This isn't business.'

'Isn't it? You married me to retain your family's company, Isla. What is that if not business?'

Her jaw hardened, frustration glittering in her eyes. 'Just give me the damn papers.'

'Only if you give me what I want.'

'But you won't tell me what you want.'

'You know already, Snow White. I told you.'

She looked like she wanted to spit something at him, and he was already relishing the fight. Instead, she looked away for a moment and when she glanced back, she was once more cold, all the liquid sapphire in her eyes hardening into glittering gems.

'Fine,' she said. 'Have it your way.' She leaned forward into the space between them and stuck out her chin. 'Come on, here I am. Take your kiss.'

Then she closed her eyes.

Orion stared at her for a long moment, conscious of a certain dark hunger stirring inside him. A hunger he'd thought he'd long since cut out of his soul.

A hunger to show her that he too could come alive if certain conditions were met, and that he too could make her fascinated with him the way he was fascinated with her.

She didn't like him, she'd been very clear on that. But she didn't need to like him in order to be fascinated with him, and he was tired of that fascination all being one way.

He could show her passion too, and it wasn't in paint or brushstrokes.

Slowly, he reached out and took her rounded little chin between his fingers and held it, watching her tense as he did so. But he didn't kiss her, not yet. He wanted her to look at him first.

Eventually, she let out an impatient breath and sure enough, her eyes opened. 'What are you doing? I thought you were going to take this kiss.'

'I am.' He gazed at her, relishing the soft feel of her skin beneath his fingers. Conscious of the faint, sweet scent of jasmine and vanilla. Pretty. 'Don't rush me.'

'You said you wanted easy and quick and—'

He leaned forward abruptly and covered her mouth with his, silencing whatever else she'd been going to say.

And for a second, he remained very still, aware of the softness of her mouth and her scent, the warmth of her skin where he held her. She'd gone still, too, and he could feel the tension in her. But since she hadn't pulled away, he touched her lips with his tongue, gently exploring, coaxing her to open to him. She was reluctant at first, then a sigh escaped her, and her mouth opened and he deepened the kiss, exploring her slowly. She tasted of mint and a tart sweetness that he found unexpectedly delicious so he chased it, the kiss getting hotter, deeper.

Her eyes had closed again, but this time it wasn't because she was shutting him out. He could feel the resistance bleeding out of her as she leaned into him, her lips moving against his, starting to kiss him back.

Satisfaction hit him like a gut punch. Ah, there it was, that passion, that life. He'd seen it sparking in her eyes and now he could taste it in her kiss. She wasn't at all cool now, was she? And one other thing was also clear: she hadn't loved her fiancé. Because if she had she wouldn't now be kissing him, another man, on her wedding day.

Orion released her chin, allowing his fingers to stroke down the silky warmth of her neck before gently circling her throat, letting his hand rest there so she was aware of it.

She tasted so good and he wanted more, and he could take it, he knew. She'd let him. But he was aware all of a sudden that he was tired of taking things. He wanted something to be given to him for a change. So after a moment, he took his hand away and lifted his mouth from hers.

Her lashes rose, her blue eyes deep as a midsummer night.

'You can have the papers,' he said, his voice rougher than he would have liked. 'But if you want anything more… Well. Let's just say I'm open to negotiations.'

Then he pulled back from her completely, tossed the papers onto the seat beside her, then rose and went down the back of the plane where he could tie up the loose ends that needed tying up without any more distractions from his new wife.

CHAPTER THREE

THE FLIGHT TO ICELAND wasn't long and Isla spent it going over the fine print of the agreement Orion had tossed at her, not to mention trying very hard not to think about the kiss he'd bargained out of her. The kiss she'd given him thinking it was only a kiss, light and fleeting and forgettable. Very much like the kiss he'd given her during their wedding ceremony.

Except it hadn't been either light, or even forgettable.

The print of Orion's agreement blurred in front of her as she remembered again the heat of his mouth and the taste of him, a hot, dark flavour with a spice to it that had taken her utterly by surprise. She hadn't known she'd find the taste of a man delicious. She hadn't known that the stroke of his tongue and the touch of his fingers could make her tremble.

Gianni, of course, had kissed her, but they hadn't slept together and neither of them had been in a hurry to do so. She'd been fine with that. In fact, she'd been relieved that she hadn't felt that same restlessness, that same electricity, around him that she felt when she was around Orion. It was dangerous that electricity. It made her feel out of control, made the flame in her heart burn hot, made her feel…hungry.

She didn't want to feel like that, especially now when she had most of the things she'd once hungered for. A home. A purpose. A future.

Not a family, though. Not someone who cares for you. Not someone to belong to.

She gritted her teeth, ignoring that betraying little thought. This was about Orion and nothing else. Anyway, she'd kissed him because he'd demanded it and because she wasn't going to get into any ridiculous bargaining nonsense. A kiss was nothing and if it meant she'd get the agreement he'd promised her then what of it?

That it hadn't been nothing was immaterial. The less said about it the better and anyway, it wasn't going to happen again. He might be her husband, but it was in name only and that's how it would stay.

Once she'd finished going over the agreement, Isla rose from her seat and went down the back of the plane. Orion was sitting at a table covered in papers, a sleek laptop open, and he was studying the screen with the same intensity of focus that he'd directed at her just before.

She put the agreement down on the table and clutched her shawl more closely around her shoulders. 'I've looked over it,' she said crisply. 'You can send that to Kendricks' legal department for them to study too.'

Orion glanced up from his screen and raised one black brow. 'You don't trust my word that it's fine?'

'No. I wouldn't trust you as far as I could throw you.'

'A wise decision.' He glanced back down at his computer screen in obvious dismissal. 'I'll send it to them.'

'Why did you want to marry me?' she asked abruptly, since it was time he started answering some of her questions and she was tired of being in the dark. 'Because if it was Kendricks' you wanted, you could have just taken it.'

He didn't look up. 'I didn't, because it wasn't Kendricks' I wanted.'

Her. He'd wanted *her*.

A tiny shock arrowed down her spine. 'That's not an answer.'

'Sadly, it's the only one you're getting. I'm extremely busy, Snow White. Why don't you go back to your seat and read a magazine or something.'

Isla gritted her teeth. 'Snow White? Really?'

His gaze remained on the screen and he said nothing, but his mouth quirked. She couldn't help looking at it. His bottom lip was full and beautifully carved. It had felt soft on hers and yet there had been a firmness to it, an insistent demand…

The electricity that hummed beneath her skin turned into a wash of heat, making her breath catch.

Why had he wanted her? What was it that had made him promise to buy an entire company just so he could marry her?

'If you're not going to read a magazine,' Orion murmured, 'you're quite welcome to stand there for the rest of the flight looking at my mouth. I don't mind. Though I warn you, I might expect something for the privilege.'

The heat reached her cheeks, making her blush, and she suddenly wanted to shake him in some way, make him as restless and unsettled as he made her. It had been going on for months now and she was tired of it. Except she didn't know how she could. He was one of the most successful corporate raiders in the world, a stone-cold, razor-sharp businessman, while she was only the adopted daughter of the Kendricks' Family Christmas CEO. The adopted daughter who'd been all potential and nothing else.

David should have returned you. That's what he should have done.

No, she could still realise that potential. Orion had promised she'd be CEO. She could still show David that his decision to adopt her thirteen years ago had been the right one. She just had to stop letting her more…intense feelings get in the way of making decisions that were good for the business. Being sympathetic to unhappy staff working long hours on a minimum wage and wanting to help them was all well and good, but paying more meant more expenses for the company, which the board didn't like.

They hadn't been happy either with her informing her father that while the factory that made the Christmas decorations might have been cheap, it also contravened several labour laws and put people's lives in danger, and so they needed to change to a different supplier. Yes, it was more expensive, but could you really put a cost on people's lives?

Apparently you could and they hadn't liked her arguing with them about it.

So now that's what she needed to learn. To put her sympathies aside. To become harder, colder. To become more ruthless.

You could try learning from him.

Now, *that* was a good idea. He was certainly hard and cold, not to mention extremely ruthless. She didn't like the thought of admitting that she needed to learn anything from him, but if she wanted to make her father proud, she had to do something.

She very much wanted to shock Orion in some way before that, though. He'd been in charge from the moment he'd walked into the church and she was tired of it.

'If you want another kiss,' he murmured without looking up. 'Please don't hesitate to ask. Though, as I said, I'll probably want something more in return for one this time.'

Something more...

Another wash of heat swept through her, her mind reeling at the thought of the 'more' he might want.

But no, thinking those things was reckless of her, dangerous even.

To stay in control of herself, she had to take control of the situation, not let him get the upper hand. And well, he was a man who took what he wanted, or so he'd said, so why couldn't she? Why couldn't she take from him? Give him a taste of his own medicine? Had anyone ever done that to him? She was thinking not.

'Orion,' she said softly.

And was gratified when he looked up. In the dim lighting of the plane, his dark golden eyes met hers and they gleamed. As if he knew already what she was about to do.

He didn't, though, she was sure. He was far too satisfied with himself, far too pleased that his little threat had worked. He thought he had her exactly where he wanted her, and well, she'd show him.

Isla reached down and grabbed him by the tie, then she bent and kissed him.

He stiffened in surprise, but didn't pull away. His mouth was firm and warm and within moments she was already half-desperate for the taste of him again. She touched her tongue to his lips the way he had with her not an hour or so ago, wanting entry.

He didn't give it.

Isla made a frustrated sound, because that wasn't fair. All she wanted was another taste; that wasn't so much to ask for was it? She traced his bottom lip with her tongue and then nipped it. She wasn't experienced, and she'd certainly never had this kind of kiss with Gianni, but then, she'd never wanted to. She'd never been as desperate to taste him as she was to taste Orion.

She wasn't expecting it when he opened his mouth slightly, turning the kiss just as hot as it had been before. Yet this time there was a wild element to it. Something raw and burning. It was thrilling and scary, and she wanted to—

Orion pulled back abruptly and she was left clutching empty air.

'Well,' he murmured, his eyes gone a brilliant, lambent gold. 'Aren't you full of surprises?'

She let go of his tie, her hands shaking, her heart beating far too fast and far too loud.

That was a mistake.

Very much so. She'd almost lost herself that time and she couldn't do that. She knew what happened when she let her hunger for what she wanted overcome her control. She ended up losing everything.

She straightened, not letting even a hint of how he'd affected her show. 'Don't get ahead of yourself, Mr North. I only wanted you to know that I can also take what I want, when I want it.'

He smiled, predatory and dangerous and everything in her tightened. 'You didn't love him at all, did you?'

A hot flush of shame washed through her, but not for Gianni's sake. They both knew she didn't love him. No, the shame she felt was for her father and the plans he'd made for her. The plans she'd agreed on that now lay in ruins, and all because of her.

But there hadn't been another choice. Orion hadn't given her one.

Or perhaps there was and you just didn't see it?

She ignored that thought and since there was nothing else she could say to that, she turned her back on him and returned to her seat.

Orion tried to work, tried to put the puzzle of his new wife out of his head, but try as he might, he couldn't.

It was a first not to be able to stop thinking of a woman. Normally, he had no trouble whatsoever. His lovers never impinged on his day-to-day life because he made sure that they didn't. He paid attention to them when he was with them, but when he wasn't, it was out of sight, out of mind.

He didn't want anyone to be important to him, because once someone became important, that's when they had power over you. That's what had happened with Cleo and their baby, and he'd never do it again. Not after that baby was taken from him.

His son. Luke.

Luke would be twenty now and what he was doing, God only knew. Orion didn't and neither did he want to, not after the decision he'd made years earlier. He'd been twenty-six and had already made the first major deal of his career, and finally he'd had the money and the power to take his son back from those who'd kept him.

He'd hired the best lawyers and filled a car full of toys, and he'd arrived at Cleo's chic little Chelsea townhouse. She'd married a tech company CEO and was now living in the manner to which she'd become very much accustomed.

It had been Luke's tenth birthday and a party was being held, with lots of people going in and out. He'd told the lawyer to wait in the car and he'd gone in alone. He'd wanted to confront Cleo personally, tell her he wasn't sixteen any longer, that he had money now, and if she wouldn't give him his son back, Orion would take him.

But he'd come through the light, airy hallway and out into the back garden, and into the cheerful chaos of a kid's birthday party in full swing. Luke was standing at a picnic table, a huge cake in the shape of some superhero or other on the top of it and everyone was singing 'Happy Birthday'. Then he bent to blow out the candles and they all cheered. Cleo's husband leaned down to say something to him and Luke laughed. Cleo's hand was on Luke's shoulder and in amongst the happy kids, he saw Cleo's father also smiling.

God, how he'd hated Cleo's father.

But all that really mattered was Luke, and his son was also smiling. His son was laughing. His son was happy. His son had everything Orion had never had himself and yet had always wanted to give him.

Orion had stood for a moment in the hallway, watching as the boy he hadn't seen since he was a baby, and only in photos since, turned ten years old. Surrounded by his family and his friends. And Orion had known there and then that he couldn't do it.

He couldn't rip his child away from the only home the boy had ever known, to go and live with the father he'd never met. The father he didn't even know he had, since Cleo had made it very clear that it would be better for Luke if he didn't know of Orion's existence.

Orion couldn't take Luke away from his family and his friends. His mother and his grandparents. The people who'd brought him up, just because he was Orion's son and Orion wanted him.

It wasn't right and he couldn't do it.

So he'd turned around and walked out of that house, and he'd never gone back.

His heart had been ripped out of his chest the day Cleo's father had told him he wasn't to have any contact with Cleo or Luke ever again, and yet some piece of it had still remained inside him.

But in that hallway in Chelsea, he'd cut out that last remaining piece. Luke was happy, that was all that mattered, and as for himself, well, it was easier to pretend he'd never had a son at all.

Luke was the one thing he'd let go of, because he'd had to. But afterwards, he'd decided that there would be no family for him. No more children. No wife. No happy home full of love and laughter. He'd grown up without any of that and he was fine, and besides, love was a power game, and one he'd lost, so now he simply refused to play.

Not that he was in any danger of falling in love with Isla. Marrying her had been part of Kendrick's deal and he'd agreed since it was either that or Kendrick found some other groom for her, and he hadn't been about to let that happen. Once he set his sights on a target he generally acquired it. He didn't like to lose. He'd keep her for the year specified, but then he'd divorce her, no harm done.

Slowly, he pushed shut his laptop and leaned back in his seat.

That kiss she'd given him… She'd taken him by surprise, he had to admit. He hadn't been expecting her to grab his tie, lean down and deliver a kiss just as hot as the one he'd given her. It took a lot to surprise him these days, but she'd managed it and he respected the hell out of her for it.

But she didn't know that in kissing him, she'd issued him with a challenge. A challenge that fired his blood. He was a wolf at heart and he loved the thrill of the chase, the hunt. He loved the fight, too, when he ran his prey down. But people didn't fight him the way they used to, his reputation had ensured that. They mostly just lay down and offered him their throat, which wasn't satisfying in any way.

Isla wouldn't just lie down and offer him her throat, he suspected. She would fight him and he relished the thought of that particular chase very much.

He hadn't planned on anything physical happening between them. All he'd wanted was to get close to her, talk to her, find out why a bit of paint on a board should have illuminated her so completely, and what exactly was the nature of that light inside her. But he wouldn't mind exploring their physical attraction if she was willing. And then once he'd explored that, perhaps this fascination would go away. Because he was tired of her being in his thoughts so continually.

Of course, that all depended on her wanting to stay at his lodge. He could make it difficult for her to leave physically—the lodge was remote and the weather could make transport to and from it tricky—but it would be much more satisfying if she chose to stay.

He could make her choose that. His new wife might look like a snow maiden, but her kiss was full of heat, and that had set him thinking about her fiancé and whether he'd been able to satisfy her and the answer was potentially not, since she'd been able to kiss another man not once, but twice. Three times if you counted the kiss at the altar.

Perhaps he'd find that out too. It had been a long time since a woman had obsessed him in such a way and now with physical chemistry added to the equation, he wasn't about to let her go anytime soon. Not until he'd exhausted his interest.

Orion spent the rest of the short remaining flight time tying up some loose ends and then making a few plans. He sent off the agreement to the Kendricks' lawyers as promised, and then made a few calls to his PR department. His shock wedding would attract some media attention, but if they stayed in Iceland long enough, the fuss would die down. Not that he particularly cared about it, but Isla might.

Soon enough, the jet began to descend into Reykjavik. Once they'd landed and the formalities were dealt with, they then boarded the helicopter that would take them to the lodge.

It was far to the south and east of the country, the lodge built at the edge of a small lake and surrounded by mountains and woodland that he was in the process of regenerating.

He had a few lodges scattered around the globe, but the one in Iceland was his favourite simply because it was so remote and wild. The ruggedness of the landscape and the changing shape of it due to the constant, churning volcanic activity appealed to him. He appreciated nature's power and how small humanity seemed against it, and ultimately how powerless.

It was a bracing perspective and he liked that.

The flight there was a spectacular one, but since it had darkened into night since they left the UK, there was no view to take in. Isla didn't say a word and kept her gaze on the blackness outside the helicopter window the whole time.

It didn't matter. They'd have plenty of time to talk when they arrived.

Luckily the weather was still and Orion had had

the helipad cleared of snow so there were no issues with landing. It was freezing outside, though.

He opened the door and helped her out, the icy air immediately catching them. She gave a little gasp and shuddered, clutching her shawl around her.

It was snowing now, and in the lights coming from the lodge and from the lit stone path that led to the front door he could see snowflakes catching her hair and on her gown, glittering and sparkling.

She looked even more like a snow maiden than ever.

She also looked as if she was freezing to death.

Before he could think better of it, he murmured, 'Come here, Snow White,' and swept her up into his arms. 'I'm supposed to carry you over the threshold.'

'No.' She'd gone stiff as a board. 'I don't want you to carry me.'

'You're freezing and your shoes are going to get wet.' He settled her more firmly against him as he turned towards the lodge. 'Also, I'm cold too and I could use the extra warmth.'

There was a fiercely resistant look on her pretty face, yet her body slowly relaxed against his. Clearly the cold had overcome her pride. 'Don't take this as a sign I like you,' she said. 'Because I don't.'

'Noted.' The tart note in her voice made him smile as he strode along the lit stone path that led to the huge wooden double front doors of the lodge. 'Tomorrow we can discuss why exactly you don't like me.'

'No, we can't.'

He glanced down at her, amused that despite her grumpy tone, she'd somehow nestled even closer. She was very warm in his arms, the scent of her body sweet in the frigid night air.

'We don't have to discuss anything if you don't want to,' he said, purely to annoy her. 'You can try and take some more kisses from me instead.'

She gave a little snort, but even in the darkness he could see her blush.

He'd had the staff member who managed the property prepare the lodge for their arrival, and the woman was there to open the big wooden double front doors for them. He stepped into the welcome warmth of the flagstone entrance way, the door shutting firmly on the arctic winter night.

He didn't pause, heading straight into the lounge to the right of the front doors. It was a vast area with big floor-to-ceiling double-glazed windows that looked out over the lake. The floor was rustic wood overlaid with thick rugs and a huge fire burned down one end. There were a couple of low sectional couches upholstered in pale leather and a low coffee table that had been rough-hewn out of a piece of pale wood and the top sanded smooth.

He carried Isla over to the couch near the fire and put her down so she could get warm, then he went to see the property manager to make sure the luggage had been unloaded and everything had been prepared to his liking. Once that had been sorted and the woman had left in the helicopter back to Reykjavik, he went back into the lounge.

Isla had slid off the couch and was sitting on her knees in front of the fire, her hands stretched out towards the blaze. She still had her shawl around her shoulders and the snow that had settled on her and her gown had melted, leaving her hair and the silk of her dress sodden.

His snow maiden melting in the heat.

An unexpected and unwelcome protectiveness rose inside him and before he could stop himself, he said, 'You need to get out of that gown and into a hot shower, and then put on something warm.'

'Love to,' she muttered, not moving. 'But I don't have any clothes with me since I wasn't exactly expecting to be taken to Iceland on my wedding day.'

'Then isn't it a good thing then that I had your luggage put on the jet when we left England?' he said. 'It's upstairs in your room now.'

'Of course you did.' She looked at him, her lush mouth trying very hard to compress itself into a firm line. 'Though I'm not sure my bikinis will be useful what with all the snow.'

He smiled. 'Oh, you'd be surprised. Come. Let me show you upstairs to your room before you freeze to death.'

'I'm quite happy here, thank you.'

'Isla.' He pitched his voice low and with an element of command in it, and was gratified when she blinked and looked at him. 'I know you don't like me, you've made that clear, but this is childish. You're cold.'

Anger flared briefly in her dark blue eyes then she looked away, long golden lashes veiling her expression. 'Fine.' The word was determindedly neutral. 'Show me where my room is then.'

Interesting how she simply shut away her emotions. Interesting too to note that she hadn't shut them away completely, because the stain of annoyance lingered in her cheeks and her shoulders were tense.

He was reminded again of a fizzing champagne bottle imperfectly capped, though that implied light bubbles of joy and she wasn't fizzy like that. She was more like a volcano, with fires burning hot and slow deep inside. A woman of passion. And a woman who had difficulty keeping that passion locked down.

You could let that passion out. You could make it explode.

Oh, he certainly could, and he was starting to think that maybe he would. Her kiss still burned on his tongue, the taste of her as sweet as her scent.

He'd like another, a deeper taste.

He kept all these thoughts from his face as he turned and led her up the rustic wooden stairs to the second floor where the bedrooms were located. He'd made sure she'd been given one of the large rooms at the end of the hall that looked out over the lake.

Inside was a rustic-looking four-poster bed hung with curtains and piled with pillows, and a white faux fur bedspread. There were rugs on the floors, the thick pale curtains pulled across the windows to shut out the freezing night.

His property manager had already unpacked for her and a delicate white lace nightgown that seemed to be sheer all the way down was laid out on the bed.

A nightgown for a wedding night.

He found himself staring at it. She had been going to wear that for Gianni...

She could wear it for you.

Heat burst through him, so intense he had to grit his teeth as she brushed past him on her way into the room, engulfing him in her sweet scent. Then she, too, stopped, staring at the nightgown. A fierce blush stained her cheeks. She darted forward and snatched the sheer bit of nothing from the bed. 'Obviously I'm not going to wear that,' she muttered.

Orion was conscious that the best thing for both of them was to let her have her shower and get changed. Now that he had her here, there was no rush for anything more quite yet.

Instead, he leaned against the doorframe and said, 'Oh? Why not?'

She didn't look at him, moving over to the bags at the foot of her bed and dumping the nightgown into one of them. 'Because it's for my wedding night and I'd hardly call this an actual wedding night.'

He watched her, swathed in her damp gown, the ends of her shawl trailing, soft golden curls coming down from her wilting up-do. Not at all the polished bride she'd been in the church, but a more rumpled, sexier and altogether more touchable version of her.

'I can give you one, though,' he said, very unwisely. 'If you want one.'

CHAPTER FOUR

ISLA STILLED. HIS VOICE was soft and very dark and not at all cold. Not this time.

Her heartbeat had accelerated and her cheeks felt hot, the embarrassment at having that ridiculous nightgown spread out on the bed so blatantly lingering.

She'd bought it for herself in a fit of optimism, because despite her misgivings, she thought she should have something sexy and beautiful to wear for her wedding night. Something that her new husband would enjoy too, though she'd expected Gianni to be that husband.

Not Orion North.

She was very conscious of him leaning in the doorway, one shoulder hitched against the doorframe, his gaze on hers. She could still feel the hard warmth of his chest as she'd lain against it on the walk from the helicopter into the lodge.

Being carried by him was the last thing she wanted, especially after those kisses, but he hadn't given her a choice. Yet the worst thing had been that once she'd found herself in his arms, she hadn't wanted to leave them. He'd been so very warm and the night had been so cold, and he'd smelled good, that dark, spicy scent of his surrounding her. And all she'd been able to think about was how delicious he'd tasted on the jet and how she wanted more.

You want more than his kiss.

She stared down at the nightgown she'd dropped into the bag at her feet. Her wedding dress felt damp and despite the room's warmth, she was shivering. But it wasn't all due to the cold.

Slowly, she turned to look at him.

He hadn't moved, his tall, powerful figure utterly still. But the glow in his wolf's eyes stole her breath. He'd looked at her that way back in the church and then just as he was about to kiss her in front of the altar.

He wants you.

A shiver stole through her.

'Well?' he prompted softly.

'A wedding night,' she said. 'Is that for me or for yourself?'

His eyes glinted. 'A very astute question. Let's just say I wouldn't be unmoved by it.'

Her mouth felt dry. He was like this in the boardroom meetings she'd been in with him, his posture relaxed, his tone casual. He was a master gambler with a true poker face, never letting a hint of his true thoughts or feelings escape.

A panther lying in wait. A wolf stalking his prey. He was stalking her now; she could feel it.

That electricity was back as it always was whenever she was near him, humming and crackling over her skin. Maddening, relentless and also wildly exciting.

Why not a wedding night with him? What would you have to lose? Perhaps if you sleep with him, this feeling will finally leave you alone.

A tempting thought and yet so dangerous. Those kisses up in the plane had made the whole world fall away, stoked the flame in her heart, and she was half afraid of what his touch would do to her. Especially when his very presence made her unsettled and angry.

He made her feel volatile and she didn't like that. Being volatile had caused her so many problems in the past. Because David hadn't been the first person who'd wanted to adopt her. There had been another couple. They'd already had a son and now longed for a daughter. She'd been ten and thrilled to be given a home, except their son hadn't been thrilled. He'd hated her from the moment she'd arrived and seemed determined to keep hating her, no matter how friendly she'd been. She hadn't wanted to upset anything and lose her home and her new-found family, so she'd tried her best to fit in and to not make things difficult.

Her new brother never hurt her, but he consistently made life difficult, breaking things and making messes and blaming them on her. She hadn't argued. She hadn't wanted to rock the boat. Yet the unfairness of it burned in her heart. She'd been there six months when one day he scratched his father's prized new car and told his parents that she'd done it. They'd been angry, unable to understand why she kept doing these things when all they'd done was give her a home. And that day she'd had enough. She'd told them that none of it had been her fault, that he'd scratched the car not her, and that he didn't like her and he didn't want her there, and that it wasn't fair. She'd been so angry.

They hadn't believed her and they'd called the social workers the next day, telling them to halt the adoption process. That it wasn't going to work out.

It had hurt. It had hurt to have the family she'd wanted so much snatched away, but she knew she only had herself to blame. Perhaps if she hadn't said anything, if she'd just kept on accepting the blame it would have been okay. Perhaps that boy would have grown out of taunting her, perhaps he would have grown to like her, but she'd never got the chance to find out, because her anger at the unfairness of it had erupted and turned everything to ashes.

Even now, it still hurt to think of it. The shame of being returned like an unwanted pet, and the frustrated fury at how it had all gone down. Fury at that boy and the adults who hadn't believed her, and most of all at herself for losing her temper. She shouldn't have been so caught up in her own feelings that she lost sight of what was important. A family and a place to belong.

But you don't even have that now though, do you? You never belonged to David or Gianni, and you don't even belong at Kendricks'. You don't belong anywhere.

Isla shoved that thought away and turned to face Orion, her heart thudding hard in her ears. Answers, that's what she needed now, not passion.

'Why did you marry me, Orion?' she asked abruptly. 'What was so important about me that you felt the need to pay off Gianni and buy Kendricks' in order to have me? I need an answer.'

He didn't reply for a long moment, still staring at her, the weight of his gaze driving all the breath from her lungs. 'I saw an opportunity,' he said at last. 'And I took it.' He pushed himself away from the doorframe and took a step into the room. 'Do you remember that function at the National Gallery? Some fundraiser, I think it was.' He took another step, full lazy, predatory grace.

Isla stared at him, her heartbeat getting louder, electricity prickling everywhere. Of course she remembered that fundraiser, how could she not?

Sometimes, when she'd been a kid and things had been difficult at whichever foster home she'd been in, she would slip away to a gallery or a museum and spend time looking at beautiful things. It was a cheap way to distract herself, and art especially was her favourite.

She shouldn't have sneaked away that night at the National Gallery, because her attendance had been required. Yet there had been a special Van Gogh exhibition on, and she hadn't been able to resist the temptation of looking at one of her favourite paintings.

'Yes,' she said. 'I remember.'

'I found you looking at *Starry Night*,' he murmured and took another step, getting closer. 'I asked you what you found so interesting about it and you told me.' Another step. He was so tall, she felt dwarfed by him. 'You talked about the paint, and the layers and the brush strokes. You talked about movement and luminosity.' Another step. His eyes had gone from dark amber to brilliant gold. 'But the most luminous thing in the gallery that night was you.' A final step brought him so close she could feel his heat, smell his scent. 'And I want to know why.'

Her heartbeat was frantic now, the electricity between them morphing into a delicious kind of exhilaration. It was such a strange feeling, almost akin to fear, though not fear for her life or that he'd hurt her. More the kind of fear you experienced being on an extremely fast roller-coaster, knowing you couldn't get off and that the only thing you could do was surrender to the moment and the breathless excitement of it all.

The only other time she'd felt that same thrill was standing in front of a particularly beautiful painting. Getting lost in the colour, becoming absorbed by the layers of paint and the brushstrokes and the play of light...

She'd known who he was when he'd entered the small gallery—most people in the business sector know who Orion North was—though they'd never actually met. She'd felt vaguely unsettled by his presence and her instant, electric response to him, and she'd been trying to think of a way to leave without being too offensive, when after a moment's tense silence, he'd asked her about the painting.

It had been the last thing she'd expected and had been so surprised, she'd answered him. She hadn't talked about art to anyone before and so had been hesitant to talk about it with a complete stranger. Yet he'd remained silent, and because she hadn't liked the silence, she'd started to speak. Then, before she knew what she was doing, she'd shared everything she knew about it and that was a lot since she researched all her favourite artists and paintings extensively.

He hadn't said a word the whole time, though she'd felt him watching her. And when she'd finished, all he'd said was, 'Fascinating.' Then he'd turned his back on her and walked out.

She'd felt like an idiot in that moment, as if she'd shown him something precious and he'd crushed it under his foot.

She stared up at him now, remembering that feeling, wanting to step back and put some distance between them, yet also bizarrely wanting to get closer.

'You remembered?' she asked stupidly. 'I thought I'd bored you.'

'You didn't bore me.' He was staring at her with such intentness she could barely breathe. 'Quite the opposite in fact.'

'But…' Her heart was beating even faster now. 'You just…walked away.'

'Of course, I walked away.' He lifted a hand and casually pulled one of the pins in her hair out and dropped it. 'It was either that or demand to know why you were the most luminous thing in the whole damn gallery.' He pulled out another pin. 'I didn't think you'd appreciate that.'

She should stop him. She should tell him to leave her hair alone, that she could take out her own pins, but she couldn't seem to form the words.

He'd thought she was luminous…

No one had ever thought she was that. Too volatile. Too quiet. Too obedient. Lots of potential. But never *luminous*…

'So you married me for…that?' She couldn't keep the raw husk of emotion out of her voice. 'I don't understand.'

'Like I told you.' He calmly took another pin out and then another. 'When I see an opportunity to acquire something I want, I take it.'

'So I'm an acquisition?' Freed from its pins her hair was starting to slip out of the carefully constructed wedding up-do. 'Like a company you target?'

'Yes.' Carefully he lifted both hands and threaded

his fingers through her hair, combing through it so her curls tumbled to her shoulders and down her back. A quiver ran through her. 'I take companies and examine them. Then I dismantle them and figure out what's working and what isn't, what's broken and what's not. What parts to keep and what to get rid of. That's why I told David I wanted to marry you. I'm hoping that once I dismantle my fascination with you, I'll finally be able get rid of it.'

Her breath had gone and all she was aware of was the pull of his fingers in her hair and how much she liked it. How much she liked being a fascination to him too, especially after years of being only a source of disappointment.

'Seems extreme.' She made no move away from him even though she knew she should. 'To pay off my fiancé and do a deal with my father to buy a whole company in exchange for me.'

His mouth curved. 'I'm not a man known for moderation when it comes to business. All or nothing, Snow White.' His fingers curled into her hair, holding her in a gentle grip. It was possessive that grip, and she found it unspeakably erotic. 'I don't regret paying off your fiancé—he accepted my money without protest which only goes to prove he wasn't good enough for you. And since buying Kendricks' was the only way I could get you, I had to buy it. I'm not a man who likes to lose.'

Her heart was beating way too fast. 'It was leverage too, wasn't it? To get me to do what you wanted.'

'Yes. But…perhaps, I regret the threat to Kendricks'.'

She stared up into his amber eyes, part of her angry with him for his sheer arrogance, part of her fascinated. She hadn't known, had barely even dreamt that anyone, let alone a man as powerful as Orion North, would want her so badly he'd do all of that just to have her. 'Do you really regret it?'

His faint smile deepened. 'No.'

She wasn't sure why she liked the combination of that rueful smile and the heat in his eyes. It softened his hard, handsome features, making him seem more approachable, not to mention even more devastatingly attractive. It made her want to smile too, which was odd given he'd threatened her into marriage for nothing more than some strange fascination with her.

She shouldn't smile at him. She shouldn't find his hands in her hair so breathtakingly erotic either, yet she did.

No one had ever found her fascinating. She'd been chosen twice and both times the people who'd chosen her had regretted their choices, first that family, and then David. Orion wasn't disappointed though, not given the way he was looking at her. As if she was the most important discovery he'd ever made.

Give him time.

No, she wasn't going to think about that. There was only this moment and the expression in his eyes and she could enjoy that, couldn't she?

'Well?' he murmured. 'Have you considered my

wedding night offer? I should very much like to see you in that nightgown. Seems a waste not to wear it.'

She shouldn't. She barely knew him and she certainly didn't like him, and the thought of sleeping with him filled her with a certain trepidation. Then again, this electricity between them wasn't going away anytime soon and she needed it to, especially when it was affecting what she did in the boardroom. Perhaps spending the night with him would be enough to get rid of it.

It's not just about the electricity. You want him.

She couldn't deny it. She'd never met another man who made her feel the way he did. And she was tired of feeling like a massive disappointment. Tired of trying to fulfil the potential her father saw in her. Tired of trying to be something she suspected she wasn't.

Why couldn't she have something for herself for a change? That was allowed, wasn't it? Just one night. He wanted her and it was thrilling to be wanted. It was thrilling to be able to put that look in his eyes, to fascinate such a powerful, ruthless man.

She'd been starting to think lately that she wasn't good at anything she did, but if she could fascinate Orion North, then maybe she wasn't as bad as she'd thought.

She wasn't just going to give in, though. He'd liked it when she'd taken that kiss from him in the plane; she knew he had. He'd liked that she'd surprised him. She wanted to keep doing that.

'Let me go,' she said quietly, making her decision.

He didn't say anything as he released his hold on her hair, but she could see the flicker of disappointment in his eyes.

Good. Let him be disappointed.

Without a word, she went to the bag where she'd put the nightgown and retrieved it. Then she moved over to the bed and laid the nightgown down on it again. 'You'll need to help me with my zip,' she said and turned around, presenting her back to him.

There was a moment of silence.

He moved so silently she didn't hear him and she only knew he was near when she felt warmth behind her, the dark spice of his scent wrapping around her, and then the tug of his fingers on her zip.

'Are you going to tease me?' His voice was full of heat and gravel. 'Because if so, I should warn you, I like to tease back.' As if to demonstrate, he drew down the zip of her gown with aching slowness, making her very aware of every inch of skin that was revealed as the material parted.

She didn't know what to say in response to that, because her voice had vanished. She felt hot, awareness of him prickling over her, humming and crackling like static.

This was madness, but she wasn't going to stop.

He was right. She'd bought that nightgown for a reason and it hadn't been Gianni she'd been thinking of when she'd bought it. Not that she'd been thinking of Orion specifically, but she'd been thinking of a man. A man who'd take a *lot* of pleasure at seeing her in it and how much that would please her too.

She moved away and allowed the gown to slide down her body and pool at her feet. Then she stepped out of the fabric, wearing only a white lace bra, knickers, stockings and heels. She wasn't quite brave enough to undress while facing him, so she kept her back to him as she kicked off her shoes, eased down her stockings, unclipped her bra and then stepped out of her knickers.

He was utterly silent, though she could feel him watching her. It made her heart race.

She reached for the nightgown. The white silk lace was sheer all the way to the hem and it hid nothing. It was designed purely to enflame.

Isla put it over her head, shivering as the cool material slid down over her skin. She adjusted the straps a little and then paused to gather her courage.

She was going to take what she wanted. And she wanted this. She wanted her wedding night and she wanted it with Orion.

Slowly, she turned around.

Orion had thought it would be easy to wait until his new wife made a decision about his offer of a wedding night. It had no doubt been a mistake to offer it in the first place, but that nightgown had decided him.

It was an opportunity.

He'd known she wanted him. He'd tasted her hunger in her kiss, and that sexy little nightgown had definitely been chosen with passion in mind. Why couldn't she experience some of that passion with him?

So he'd put the offer out there to see what she did with it.

He'd expected her to turn him down immediately and when she hadn't, he couldn't stop himself from stalking over to her. He'd wanted to see what was going on in that pretty head of hers, wanted to see the sparks in her deep blue eyes, and sure enough they'd been there.

Perhaps it had been unwise of him to let her know how much she'd fascinated him that day in the National Gallery, but when she'd asked him directly why he'd married her, he hadn't been able to lie to her.

It wasn't as if he was confessing to a lifelong passion, after all. Merely a fascination that he would soon deal with. A fascination he would take apart to see how it worked and he'd then get rid of it.

He hadn't thought he'd be impatient for an answer to his wedding night offer. He hadn't thought it would matter to him. Yet he'd found himself unable to stop touching her, taking the pins from her hair and running his fingers through all the soft golden curls. Watching her eyes darken as they looked up into his and the pulse at the base of her throat race.

Oh, yes, she wanted him, that was undeniable.

Which had then made her request to stop touching her so very disappointing.

In fact, he'd been surprised by how disappointed he was. She might want him, but he hadn't realised the full extent of his own hunger for her.

He'd told himself it didn't matter, that he didn't care, and then she'd picked up that damn nightgown, gone over to the bed and laid it down. Then she'd turned her back on him and requested help with her zip.

Apparently, she wasn't saying no after all.

Something savage had filled him in that moment, triumph and satisfaction and hunger all mixed into one. The intensity of it had disturbed him since he reserved all his passions for the boardroom not the bedroom.

He enjoyed sex but he never lost himself to it. He couldn't afford to. His control over himself, both emotionally and physically, was vital and he kept himself in hand at all times. Besides, sex simply wasn't important enough to him to be worth the risk of an unwanted pregnancy.

Apparently, though, all of that didn't matter as he slowly undid the zip on Isla's dress and all that smooth, pale porcelain skin came into view. Watching as her wedding dress slipped slowly from her, revealing rounded thighs, generous hips and a small waist.

And all his control was worth nothing because the only thing he could think about was grabbing

her by those luscious hips and simply flinging her
on the bed.

Covering herself with the nightgown didn't help
and when she finally turned around to face him, he
knew the battle with himself and his control was lost.

Because he'd never seen anything so delicious
in all his life.

The nightgown clung, revealing the gorgeous
curves of her breasts and the soft pink of her nipples visible through the lace. The curls between her
thighs were visible too and they were as golden as
the hair on her head.

Her chin had lifted, her shoulders tensed, and her
gaze when it met his was defiant, though what she
was defiant about he didn't know, because there was
nothing about her that wasn't completely and utterly
delicious. And he wanted her to know that, so he let
his hunger show in his eyes.

Something ignited in her then, a blaze of heat
flushing her cheeks, making her glow, and in that
moment, he knew something true: she was his painting. She was his *Starry Night*. All curves and movement and luminous colours. Cream and gold and pink
and the deep dark blue of her eyes. She came alive
the way she had that night at the gallery as she'd
explained that painting to him. Startlingly lovely.
Luminous.

He was barely aware of moving, of striding over
to her and settling his hands on her hips, feeling the
warmth of her skin through her gown. And at the

same time, she reached for him, lifting her hands and taking his face between them.

There was no fear in her eyes, only the same hunger that burned in him, and when he bent and took her mouth, it felt like a relief. As if he'd been in the desert dying of thirst and she was his first taste of water.

She leaned into him, kissing him back the way she'd kissed him in the jet, full of an unpractised passion that had the blood surging in his veins. Briefly, it occurred to him to wonder just how experienced she was with men, then her hands fell from his face and she was winding her arms around his neck, her body pressing delicately against his and all thought left him.

He wrenched his mouth from hers, pulled her arms from around his neck and held her away from him.

She stared at him, her mouth full and red, her eyes dark. 'What?' she asked breathlessly. 'Did I do something—?'

'Hush,' he ordered, low and rough. 'And keep still. I want to look at you.'

'Oh…' She let out a breath, her cheeks flushing an even deeper pink as he let his gaze wander over that incredibly sexy nightgown, studying the delicate rose of her hard nipples and how the lace both revealed and hid those beautiful golden curls between her thighs.

He bent his head and kissed her throat, tasting her

frantic pulse before trailing his tongue down over the lace, following the curves of her breasts to tease her nipples through the fabric. She shuddered, a soft gasp escaping her, and when he took one nipple into his mouth, she groaned, arching into him.

Her heat and her scent were intoxicating, and before he knew what he was doing, he'd gone to his knees in front of her, his hands spread out on her soft hips, holding her steady as he kissed his way down her stomach to the heat between her thighs, using the fabric of her nightgown to tease both her and himself.

'Orion.' His name was a gasp as he pressed his tongue between her legs, dampening the white silk that veiled her, tasting her sweet feminine musk.

She was even more beautiful than he'd expected and suddenly he was tired of the nightgown. It had done its duty, but its role was over.

He gripped the delicate white silk in his hands and tore it open from hem to neck without a second's thought. Then he pulled away the fabric and rose to his feet once again, looking down at her nakedness.

His snow maiden was all white and pink and the most utterly delicious woman he'd ever seen.

She said nothing as he stared at her, only gave him a challenging look, as if daring him to do his worst, and of course he couldn't think of anything else he'd rather do. So he grabbed her by the hips and tossed her onto the bed, then followed her down onto it. He pinned her beneath him, covering her full mouth with his and kissing her hungrily.

She tasted hot and wild, her curvy little body shifting impatiently beneath his, and her hands were tearing at his tie and his suit jacket, trying to undo the buttons, trying to get to him.

He shifted astride her, rising to his knees and stripped away his tie, his jacket and his shirt, then he bent over her once again, kissing her deeply as her cool fingers touched his skin and he felt something shudder deep inside him.

He needed to slow down, get a handle on himself somehow, but then her hands were stroking his stomach and venturing further, getting bold as she traced the line of his erection through the material of his trousers.

Lights exploded in his head, electricity arcing down the length of his spine. He couldn't believe one touch would make him feel this way, but there was no denying he wanted her. He wanted her more than he wanted his next breath.

'So you do like to tease,' he growled against her mouth. 'Perhaps I'll repay you in kind.' Except he'd never felt less like teasing.

'No, please don't,' she whispered, arching against him. 'I just need… I need you.'

It felt good to be needed by her, so very good, and so he didn't wait.

Taking his mouth from hers, he found his wallet in the back pocket of his trousers and he extracted one of the condoms in there, because he never went anywhere without one. Then, after discarding the wallet, he pulled open his trousers and dealt with the protection before settling himself between her thighs.

He slipped one hand beneath the softness of her bottom and lifted her, tilting her hips and positioning himself. Then he thrust in hard, because he couldn't wait, not a second longer.

She gasped, stiffening beneath him and he knew a moment's shock, wondering if he'd hurt her. Then abruptly she curled one leg around his hip and lifted a hand, pushing her fingers into his hair and bringing his mouth down on hers, and the moment was gone.

There was only the wet heat of her sex gripping him so tight and the softness of her body beneath his. He moved deeper, harder, gathering her close and holding her against him, devouring her mouth before moving on to exploring her throat and the delicate structure of her collarbones.

She moaned beneath him, her hands clutching at his shoulders before stroking down his back and then up again, as if she was lost in a storm and trying to find something to hold on to. So he took her hands and held them down on the pillows on either side of her head, threading his fingers through hers and holding on as he moved faster, deeper, driving them into insanity.

There was a time for watching prey and a time for taking the opportunity to attack. And then there was a devouring and that's what he wanted now. To devour her. To devour her utterly.

And as she tensed and cried his name, her inner

muscles clenching tight around him, and he could feel the orgasm exploding along every nerve ending he had, he was exquisitely aware of one thing.

He was going to take her apart. Take her apart completely. Find out what made her tick, what made her so relentlessly fascinating to him, why it had to be her.

And he wasn't going to let her go until he did.

CHAPTER FIVE

ISLA CAME TO wakefulness slowly the next morning. She was full of a delicious lassitude, with aches in strange places, and a head full of memories from the night before that made her roll over and press her hot face into the pillow.

Orion...

Orion, and the way he'd looked at her with such ferocity. Orion, and how he'd touched her with such mastery. Of how he'd ripped apart that silly nightgown to get to her, then tossed her on the bed, unable to wait to be inside her.

She hadn't told him she was a virgin and maybe she should have, but she hadn't wanted him to stop. She hadn't wanted to get into any discussions about why and how either. She hadn't wanted anything that would interrupt the moment, especially when he'd been nothing but raw, unleashed passion. He'd been glorious and he'd made her feel glorious too. As if she'd thrown herself into the middle of a blazing fire and loved how intensely she'd burned.

He'd kept her there all night, stoking that fire over and over, making her rise like a phoenix from the ashes again and again. Exploring her body as if he was fascinated by it and wanted to discover all the ways it could bring her pleasure.

She hadn't known sex could be like that. She hadn't known she'd lose herself so completely.

You suspected, though. Which is why you can't allow it to happen again.

Something painful ached behind her breastbone, but she brushed it aside. It was true, she couldn't. One night, she'd promised herself. One night to take what she wanted and that's what she'd done. But she couldn't afford another. She couldn't let him get under her skin more than he had already, not when control over herself was already an issue for her.

And apart from anything else, they hadn't discussed what was going to happen now.

Perhaps it was simply about the sex, and now he's had you he'll put you on the first plane back to the UK.

Her stomach dropped away at the thought, which was disturbing, because why should she care? She didn't want to stay here with him. She needed to get back home and see her father. Ask him why he'd decided to agree to Orion's demand to marry her without even a word to her. It wasn't something she wanted to do, but she had to do it all the same.

You don't want to know why he thought so little

*of you that he sold you to one man, then when that
didn't work out, he sold you to another.*

But she didn't want that thought in her head, so
she pushed it away, turning to look at the pillow next
to her instead. But it was empty. She didn't know
whether to feel disappointed about that or relieved.

Regardless, there was no point lying there with
all these questions. She had to get up and confront
the man she'd married.

The bed was extraordinarily comfortable and she
was warm, and she didn't particularly want to do any
confronting right now, but there was nothing to be
gained by delaying it. So she forced herself out of
bed and into the ensuite bathroom.

There was a giant white-tiled shower with big
windows that had views over the snowy landscape
outside and Isla stood under the warm spray of
water, staring out through the glass at the winter
wonderland outside even as she relished the heat of
the shower.

After she got out and towelled herself dry, she
went over to the chest of drawers that stood near
the windows and opened them. All the clothes she'd
brought with her had been unpacked and folded
neatly, so she grabbed some jeans and an oversized
jersey in soft, light blue cashmere and got dressed.

Then she went out and down the stairs in search
of Orion.

She could smell something delicious coming from
the direction of what she assumed was the kitchen

so she followed the scent, coming out into a large and very expensively fitted out open-plan kitchen, with lots of stainless steel and white tiles. Near the windows that had that same pretty snow-covered lake view was a dining table set for two with cutlery, plates and cups. There was a coffee pot and orange juice, and various different spreads.

Clearly Orion was expecting for them to have breakfast together, though he himself was nowhere to be seen.

Puzzled, she checked the lounge area, but he wasn't there either. So she went down the hall, passing another bathroom, some more bedrooms and a cosy-looking library, and then, finally, a doorway that opened out into an office.

It had the same floor-to-ceiling windows as the rest of the lodge, but the view was out towards the mountains, ridged and sharp and capped with snow. A huge rustic-looking desk stood in front of the windows and behind the desk sat Orion. His attention was on the flat screen in front of him and he didn't look up as she entered.

She'd been subconsciously bracing herself for the reality of him after their night together, but it wasn't until that moment that she realised that bracing herself for him was impossible.

He was dressed casually, in worn jeans and a dark blue T-shirt, and his feet were bare. His black hair was slightly tousled and it was clear from the five o'clock shadow lining his strong jaw that he hadn't shaved. He looked thoroughly disreputable and so sexy her breath caught.

'Good,' he said, keeping his gaze on the screen. 'You're up. I've made breakfast for us.'

She came slowly into the room, disturbed to find the familiar fizz and crackle of electricity was prickling over her skin again. Ridiculous. Why was she still feeling it? Last night should have dealt with their physical chemistry and yet…apparently not.

Isla forced the feeling away as she approached his desk.

'I've had my PR department handle the media,' he went on before she could get a word out, 'since there was apparently quite a fuss about our wedding. I've given them a statement to send out that you and I had been pining for each other all this time, and Gianni selflessly stood aside at the last minute to allow me to marry you. Yes, it's a bit overly romantic, but the press love that kind of stuff.' He gave the mouse a decisive click. 'We'll be here for a couple of weeks and I have some excursions planned. Don't worry, you won't be bored.' He leaned back in his seat, his amber gaze meeting hers head-on. 'Any questions?'

Isla had many, *many* questions, yet the moment he looked at her, all of them went straight out of her head. He'd looked at her like this the night before, when she'd put on that nightgown and he'd stared at her, intent and utterly focused. Purposeful.

Yet she didn't want to stand there in silence. She had a plan and it didn't involve two weeks of 'excursions'.

'That sounds lovely,' she said, trying to sound cool and firm. 'But I can't stay, Orion. This isn't actually a honeymoon—I mean, our wedding wasn't even really a wedding—and I have to go home. I have to explain to the board what happened.'

Orion raised a brow. 'Explain? Explain what? Your father and I have handled it, and the board will be fine with me as Kendricks' new owner. And as far as our wedding not being a real wedding, I have the marriage certificate that proves otherwise.'

Irritation coiled inside her. '*You* and he might have handled it, but how do you think that looks to the board? I'm supposed to be the CEO at some point and yet there are already deals being done behind my back, without my knowledge.'

'As I said, I have that handled already,' Orion stated calmly. 'Besides, your father wanted you to marry someone, correct? Does it matter who?'

She wanted to tell him that of course it mattered who. Gianni had been chosen specifically because he was one of David's protégé's and well-respected by the Kendricks' board. Someone who would bolster confidence in her, not someone who might cause them to question her leadership potential. The worst thing was that Orion was probably aware of how little they thought of her already. It was why he'd targeted Kendricks'. She was a vulnerability and everyone knew it.

Tension crawled through her, acid gathering in the pit of her stomach. The lovely warmth she'd woken up with was dissipating and reality was asserting itself, the fallout of yesterday crashing down on her.

'I had to marry, Gianni,' she forced out. 'David was his mentor and he had standing with the board. It's a family company and being oriented around Christmas, that's what they require from their future CEO. A family. Me having to marry you at the last minute—'

'Was not ideal,' Orion interrupted with the same maddening calm. 'Which was why, if you'd given me a moment, I would have told you that I've also been on a video call with the board of Kendricks' this morning.'

Isla's stomach dropped away. 'What?'

'I met with them to discuss the sale of the company to me. I wanted to tell them personally. Also that I planned to keep the company intact for the next year at least, and to give them some explanation for our marriage and why it occurred in the manner it did. Be assured.'

Shock coursed through her as she stared at him. 'You couldn't have waited for me so we could have told them together?'

He only stared back, completely at his ease. 'I wanted to spare you the awkwardness of lying about how in love with me you were.'

Isla opened her mouth then shut it again, not knowing at all what to say to that.

'I know that many of them don't have confidence in you,' he went on smoothly. 'That they're concerned you don't have the backbone they need in a CEO. You're too quiet and not authoritative enough. Too much your father's yes man. And I find that puzzling because the woman I married yesterday was *all* backbone. There was nothing quiet about her when she grabbed my tie and kissed me.'

Isla could feel colour creeping up her neck and flushing her cheeks. She'd never had her weaknesses catalogued so completely one moment, before being refuted the next.

She looked away, unable to deal with the directness of his gaze, staring down at her hands clasped in front of her instead. 'That's because I was angry with you. I have to lock that down in the boardroom.'

'Why? Anger can be a useful tool if you stay in command of it.'

But that was the problem, wasn't it? She couldn't stay in command of it. She had a problem with her temper and if she wasn't careful, it got away from her. It had lost her that one family years earlier, and earned her father's disapproval when she'd first started working at Kendricks'. She'd tried to bring up the subject of lifting wages for the lower-paid workers in the company, and had been roundly dismissed by the board. And she hadn't thought. She'd argued and had ended up shouting, before leaving the room in tears. David had been horrified, but not more horrified than she was at herself. She'd kept herself under strict control ever since. Not that she was going to explain that to him.

'Yes, well, be that as it may,' she said coolly, lifting her gaze to his once more. 'It was my responsibility to speak to the board, not yours.'

He shrugged, as if it was of no consequence. 'Perhaps, but it's done now. They were happy with my explanation so there's no need for you to contact them. And our marriage is also done now.'

She wanted to shout at him, but there was nothing to be gained from it, since he was right. 'So, what? I'm just your wife for ever?'

'No. I promised your father a year. A year for you to remain as my wife. A year for you to be CEO. And a year for me to keep Kendricks' intact.'

'So what happens now?'

'What happens now is our honeymoon. We can discuss the rest later. So, I'm sorry, Isla, but I'm afraid you're staying. I have a helicopter flight planned to see some of the major volcanic sites. Also some skating on the lake. You can use your bikinis for a dip in the hot pool near the lodge, since the water is heated by a natural hot spring related to the volcanic activity in the area. I should imagine you'd like to see the northern lights too. Oh, yes, and I was thinking that we could also do an overnight trip to Amsterdam. I'm told the Van Gogh Museum is a must-see.'

The tension inside her pulled tighter. He'd taken control of the situation and of her so easily, and now she was here, in his territory, and it seemed to her as if he wasn't going to let her leave.

'Let me get this straight,' she said, ignoring him. 'You're going to keep me here in this lodge, against my will, and we're just going to...what? Go on little trips?'

He lounged back in his chair, the dark gold of his eyes gleaning wolflike in the wan, snowy light coming through the windows. 'I'm not keeping you here against your will, Snow White. You can leave at any time. However, you'll need a pilot since the lodge is only accessible by helicopter. Also, the weather forecast isn't looking good for the next couple of days, so you'll probably end up staying anyway.' He smiled faintly. 'Why not enjoy yourself while you wait?'

A shiver went through her at that smile and the suggestion of heat in his voice. Oh, yes, she could enjoy herself. Especially if it involved—

But no. She couldn't get sucked into *that* and the way he made her feel. She wasn't sleeping with him, not again. And as for the 'excursions'...

Something pulsed inside her, an ache she hadn't realised was still there. She'd been the only child of a single mother who'd died of cancer when Isla was four. Her mother had had no family and so Isla had been placed in a children's home. It hadn't been awful but it hadn't been great, either, and to distract herself, she'd often dream of what her future would look like, the places she wanted to go, and the things she wanted to do. The experiences she wanted to have.

The girl she'd been would have loved visiting a

volcano and seeing the northern lights. Going skating and lounging in a hot pool and seeing the Van Gogh Museum…

He's right. Why not enjoy yourself? Especially if you have to stay here a few days anyway.

She took a slow, silent breath. Arguing with him would only set her temper off and she couldn't afford that. So would it really be so bad to stay here with him? For a little while at least. She'd already planned for a week of honeymoon anyway so she wouldn't be losing anything. She was annoyed with how he'd taken charge, it was true, but she wasn't going to let him get his own way. She couldn't, not if she wanted to develop more of the CEO edge the board was hoping for.

Perhaps she could start that edge now. Perhaps, if he was going to demand some things of her, she'd demand something of him right back.

She eyed him. 'And what about our marriage after this so-called honeymoon is over?'

That faint smile was still playing around his mouth and she decided right there and then that she was going to knock it off his face as soon as she could. 'What about it?'

'Do I have to move in with you? Are we going to live together as husband and wife for the next year?'

'Maybe,' he said with infuriating calm. 'Or maybe we'll simply live separate lives. It depends on whether I've managed to explore our relationship to its fullest extent.'

'*You* don't get to decide that,' she snapped, losing patience and forgetting she was supposed to stay in control of her temper. 'In case you haven't noticed, I have a say in this, as well.'

'Oh, I haven't forgotten.' His cold voice was abruptly full of heat, and brilliant gold gleamed in his eyes. 'Believe me, I haven't forgotten.'

He was looking at her again that way, that fierce, intent way, and she could feel something throb deep inside her. An ache, a longing.

She liked the way he looked at her. She *wanted* it.

You can't want it too badly, and you really can't let him get under your skin.

That was true, that was a good reminder.

Isla swallowed. 'Fine. I guess since I have no choice in the matter then I'll stay. And I'll do your excursions. But I'm not sleeping with you again, Orion. And that's final.'

Orion sat behind his desk and stared at the self-contained little woman on the other side of it. Today she was in jeans and a soft-looking jersey in light blue cashmere, and her hair was hanging in the most glorious golden curls over her shoulders and down her back. The colour of her jersey highlighted the blue of her eyes and one shoulder had slipped down revealing her silky, pale skin.

He was already hard and she hadn't even got close to him.

He kept getting fixated by a couple of marks on

her neck that he'd left on her during the previous night, and finding it oddly satisfying to see them there. He also kept thinking about how he wanted to leave more, and of course she'd let him, because how could she not? When their night together had been so intense?

He'd risen early that morning to speak to the board and to organise the rest of their honeymoon, already thinking of taking her back to bed after they'd had breakfast together.

He hadn't thought that first she'd tell him she needed to return to the UK as quickly as possible, before not only looking distinctly unimpressed by the trips he'd planned, but also coolly informing him that she wouldn't be sleeping with him again.

That wasn't what he wanted. What he wanted was to get to the bottom of his fixation with her, especially now that the fixation had a physical aspect to it, and so he hadn't been able to resist goading her. He wanted to see her lose that cool of hers, especially after last night.

Oh, yes, most especially after that. He'd underestimated their chemistry considerably, which had led to a loss of control he hadn't experienced since he'd been sixteen and Cleo had first come on the scene. That had *not* ended well to say the least and he'd been adamant with himself that it would *never* happen again.

Until Isla. Until those long, hot hours he'd spent exploring her, releasing her passion again and again.

It had been addictive that passion and it had haunted him all morning. He'd been impatient in dealing with all the loose ends from their wedding and discussing the ins and outs of their marriage was the very last thing he wanted.

What he wanted was to take her to bed and explore their chemistry in greater depth, because now he'd had a taste, he couldn't wait to find out more.

Still, there was no point revealing how annoyed he was by her decision not to sleep with him again, so he only looked back at her calmly. 'Are you sure?'

'I think so.' She sounded cool and yet a deep red flush had stained her cheeks. 'It was a night to remember certainly, but I feel no need to revisit it.'

'Really?' He pushed his chair back. 'That must be why you refused to sleep until I made you come a third time. Because all your curiosity was satisfied and you feel no need to revisit it.'

Her blush deepened further and she carefully clasped her hands in front of her. 'I'm sorry if that makes you unhappy. But we made no promises to each other.'

It shouldn't matter to him. This need to keep pushing for more from her shouldn't be so intense, and he certainly shouldn't be quite *so* disappointed by her refusal. And yet...

Hunger pulled at him, along with that nagging sense of fascination. As if she was a book he was desperate to read, written in a language he couldn't quite understand, and he knew that if he studied her long enough, everything would become clear. Every secret would be revealed.

He couldn't give that up. He wouldn't. His fascination hadn't become less for having slept with her. If anything, it had become more intense, as if the night they'd shared had created some kind of bond between them, a physical bond that deepened what was already there.

The intensity of his own need was slightly unsettling, but since the whole reason she was here was so they could explore that connection, he didn't see any need to be too concerned. No doubt his obsession, if given free rein, would soon pass.

'Wrong,' he said and got to his feet. 'We certainly did make promises to each other. To love, honour and cherish, if I remember correctly. Till death do us part, et cetera.' He moved around the desk, then leaned casually back against it. Getting closer to her, but not too close, observing what his nearness did to her.

She took a half step back, the pulse at the base of her throat beating faster, and he could feel satisfaction dig its claws in. She might not want to sleep with him again, but that didn't mean he didn't affect her.

'But you didn't mean them and neither did I,' she said.

Orion folded his arms. 'How do you know I didn't mean them?'

Her eyes narrowed into thin slits of sapphire. 'So you really are going to love me for as long as we both shall live?'

Little minx. He'd known for a few months about the board's doubts in her and while initially he'd agreed with them, he wasn't so sure now. Not with the way she was looking at him, all stubborn spirit and challenge, and not at all the quiet, self-effacing woman he'd seen in the boardroom.

Now he thought about it, that was another thing he was curious about. Why she was so quiet when she was definitely not quiet in the slightest? There were so many things he wanted to know.

'Love has nothing to do with our chemistry, Isla,' he said. 'And when you were calling my name last night, you certainly meant it.' He raised a brow. 'Or perhaps you didn't. Perhaps you were faking all those orgasms I gave you.'

Her mouth compressed with obvious irritation. 'I had no idea you were so invested in sex.'

'I'm a man, Snow White. Of course I'm invested in sex. And so are you, I think. Why else are you blushing so fiercely? Why else have you taken a step back from me?' He pushed himself away from the desk and closed the distance between them, looking down into her pink face. 'It's not because you're scared of me, is it?'

Anger glittered in her eyes and she held her ground, which pleased him immeasurably. 'No, of course not. But you're overestimating your abilities in the bedroom. Or rather, my interest in them.' Then she lifted her chin and if that wasn't a direct challenge, he didn't know what was. 'I don't need any-thing from you. Not a single thing.'

Oh, she might think that. She might even believe that. But she was wrong. He'd discovered that she was a passionate woman, that she was, indeed, a volcano, and last night she'd erupted all over him. It had been an incredible experience to release that in her, to stoke her passion so intensely she hadn't been able to keep it inside. Intoxicating almost. And while she might not admit to herself that she needed that release from him, she did.

And he was willing to give it to her wherever and whenever she wanted for the next twelve days at least.

'I suppose we'll see,' he murmured. 'I have an idea that I'd like to try. As a kind of getting-to-know-you thing.'

'I don't need to get to know you.'

'Indulge me, Snow White. You might like it.'

The look she gave him was suspicious, which amused him more than it should. But all he said was, 'It's twelve days until Christmas. So, I propose that for each of those twelve days, we give each other a gift.'

A small crease appeared between her brows. 'A gift? Such as?'

'Perhaps... I could help you overcome your shortcomings with the board. Give you some ad-vice, something along those lines. And you will give me, say—'

'If it's sex,' she interrupted. 'Forget it. Don't be a cliché.'

She thought she knew him, didn't she? Well, she wasn't wrong about the sex, he did want that. But that wasn't all he wanted.

'I was thinking a kiss,' he said mildly. 'Or maybe a secret. Your presence on one of these excursions I've organised.'

She frowned. 'A secret? My presence? Why?'

'I told you last night, Isla. You are interesting to me and I want to know why. Twelve days should be enough time to figure it out and then after that, we can go our separate ways, live separate lives until the year is up.'

'So, I can give you…anything?'

'It must be something you know I'd like.'

'What about if I don't want the gift you're going to give me?'

She was sharp, he'd give her that. 'A gift once presented cannot be refused.'

'That goes for you as well?'

'Of course.' He gave her another smile. 'Except the gift of your absence is not acceptable. Once you agree to this, we'll both be bound to remain here for the twelve days of Christmas.'

For a second she said nothing, studying him, clearly turning the idea over in her head. It was good she was thinking it through. He didn't want her to dismiss it out of hand, especially because now he'd thought of it, he wanted it. He wanted it badly, and that was a dangerous thing to allow. He couldn't let it mean anything. This was just a silly game he'd proposed, nothing more, and if she refused then he'd simply figure out something else.

'And if I say no?' she asked. 'If I want to go home in a couple of days?'

Orion ignored the way his gut tightened. 'You're not a prisoner here, Isla. You can leave whenever you like.'

'Twelve days,' she mused. 'That's a long time. It's Kendricks' busy period.'

'That didn't seem to bother you when you scheduled a December wedding,' he pointed out, trying to mask his impatience. 'And a honeymoon afterwards that you were going to go on.'

She didn't say anything to that, merely chewed on her bottom lip.

Had he given away how much he wanted this? Was she drawing this out deliberately?

He didn't like that idea, not at all, so he put out a finger and touched her lip gently. 'Make a decision, Snow White,' he murmured. 'I will not wait all day.'

Her eyes went wide and she stilled, her mouth opening a little. And this time the sparks in her eyes were flames.

Oh, she wanted him all right. She could deny it all she wanted, but they both knew the truth. For a second, he debated pushing her, because her mouth was very soft and he wanted to keep touching it, but then he decided against it, taking his finger away.

He wanted a present. A gift. Christmas had never meant anything to him because he'd had no family of his own, and the foster families he'd been placed with either hadn't cared about it or only in a minimal way. No one had ever thought of giving him a Christmas gift, for example.

But if she agreed to this then she would. She would give him little presents every day, things he didn't have to ask for, things he didn't have to take. Things he wanted.

He almost couldn't bear the thought of her refusal.

To cover his impatience, he turned and went back behind his desk and sat down. He didn't look at her, directing his attention back to his email instead and continuing to work as if she wasn't still standing there and he wasn't waiting for her to agree to his terms.

There was no point pressing her. Either she said yes or she didn't. It was up to her.

After a few moments, she finally let out a breath and said, 'Fine. Twelve days.'

Orion very carefully kept the triumph from his expression and ignored completely the relief that nearly made him catch his breath. 'Good. Why don't you go and have some breakfast and think about your first gift to me? I have to finish up some work.'

CHAPTER SIX

Isla spent the rest of the day wondering what she'd got herself into. Orion didn't emerge from his office all day, which was fine because quite frankly she needed a break from his overwhelming presence, not to mention some time to think.

Despite Orion's assurances that he'd 'dealt with it', she used her phone to email David to tell him that she was okay, though she couldn't quite bring herself to confront him about the deal he'd made with Orion and why he hadn't told her about it. After all, she was the one who'd agreed to marry for the sake of the company and for David. She could hardly complain about a change of groom when she didn't have any feelings for said groom either way.

She was annoyed however when she got his reply that the board were pleased about her marriage to Orion, regardless of the impulsive nature of the wedding. They had been unsure about her being kept on as CEO, but Orion's assurances that he'd keep the company intact for the next year at least had allayed some fears.

That did not help Isla's temper. Of course the addition of a man made her being CEO much more palatable and it rankled.

She wanted to do right by David, to prove that he'd made the right choice when he'd adopted her, but his lack of support only added to the feeling that what she was doing was making things worse not better.

One thing was clear to her though; she couldn't just leave. If the board thought her marriage to Orion was a good thing, then throwing a tantrum and flying home today wouldn't help her cause. That *would* be letting her anger get the better of her and she couldn't do that.

Also, she could hardly refuse the idea of Christmas presents, since that was what Kendricks' was all about. Except Christmas for her wasn't about family—David for all that he was the 'Christmas magnate' didn't celebrate it. Not when Christmas was the busiest time work wise for them. In fact, she couldn't remember a time where he had celebrated it with her. Usually, Christmas meant donating her time to work in a homeless shelter or something similar. She didn't mind that, having come from nothing herself, but she didn't much like the cynical way David always turned it into a media circus.

Yet that was the way he ran things and she couldn't argue. She wasn't any blood of his, only the girl he'd adopted because his wife before she died had wanted him to find a daughter to leave the company to.

Not a daughter to love.

Her heart ached at that thought, but it was an old pain and so she put aside. The most important thing was how she was going to handle Orion for the next twelve days, because she was going to have to keep him at a distance, not let him get too close.

She was also going to have to figure out what to get him as a 'gift'. Not something sexual since she'd already decided she wasn't going to sleep with him again, and anyway, she didn't want to give him something he'd expect. She also didn't want to give him something that would add to the power he already had, which meant it not only had to be unexpected, but also shake that supreme confidence of his in some way.

'It has to be something you think I would like.'

Except she didn't know what he would like. She didn't know anything about him, beyond him being a ruthless corporate raider. There were bios of him floating around on the internet, but she hadn't read any of them. She'd told herself she wasn't interested. She'd heard that he'd been an orphan like she was, but again, she hadn't wanted to find out any more because she hadn't wanted to feel sympathy or kinship towards him.

Besides, what did you get a man who had everything he could ever want?

He doesn't have you.

The thought refused to go away. And even though she spent the day in the little library she'd spotted, accumulating a nice stack of books to read and distracting herself now and then with stares out the window at the beauty of the snowy landscape beyond the glass, it was still there by the time night fell.

She was curled up in one of the chairs in the library when she heard the door to Orion's office open and then sometime later, shutting again. Half of her was relieved he hadn't bothered to come and find her, while the other half was annoyed. Not that she wanted him to. Of course, she didn't want him to.

Yet that left her alone with her thoughts and the fact that if she wanted to give him something she knew he would like, it would have to be something to do with her.

It could be a secret...

She didn't have any secrets, though. There was nothing of interest about her, and why he was so fascinated with her she didn't understand. Still, she had to give him something.

That night she ate her dinner alone, then indulged in a bath in her ensuite before going to bed.

She slept like a log and when she woke up the next morning, she lay there going over what she was going to give Orion today.

Perhaps it would have to be a kiss. She didn't want to give him one, not when she knew she was too susceptible to it backfiring on her, and besides, she had to hold something back; it wouldn't do to give him everything he wanted straight away. Yet what else did she have?

When she went downstairs, breakfast was waiting for her and this time so was he, sitting at the table, casually sipping his coffee. His amber gaze was intent as it met hers and she found her heartbeat accelerating the way it always did when he was around.

He was just as gorgeous as he'd been yesterday, still dressed in jeans and a casual shirt of some soft-looking black textured fabric. The neck of the shirt was open, revealing the smooth olive skin of his throat, and she couldn't drag her gaze away from it.

She'd kissed him there that night they'd spent together and tasted the salt of his skin. The memory made her mouth go dry and her face feel hot.

As if he knew exactly what she was thinking, he gave her one of those slow-burning smiles that made her insides melt and something insistent throb between her legs. 'Good morning, Snow White.' His voice was on the edge of a purr. 'I trust you slept well.'

She pulled out the chair opposite and sat down, while he pushed a cup of coffee in her direction. 'Thank you,' she muttered, trying to calm her racing heart. 'Yes, I did.'

'I'm excited about my gift.' He took a sip of his own coffee, watching her, his dark golden eyes glinting in the cool winter sunlight coming through the windows. 'I'm assuming you've thought of something.'

Her heart was beating far too fast and she knew

abruptly that she couldn't give him the kiss she'd been planning on. If he could make her this flustered simply by looking at her, she couldn't risk a kiss. It was a loss of control she couldn't allow herself.

'Yes.' She tried to make the word calm and cool. 'I'm going to give you a secret.'

It wasn't much of a secret, but she couldn't think of anything else.

He smiled, though, and the gleam that lit in his eyes was genuine interest. It was as if she'd offered him the rarest of jewels.

He put his coffee down and leaned his elbows on the table, expression expectant. 'A secret? I'm assuming it's a secret about you?'

She blushed helplessly. 'Yes, but it's silly. It's not even a secret.'

'I'll be the judge of that.'

She sighed and glanced away, cupping her coffee mug in her hands and pressing her fingertips against the hot ceramic. He was going to be disappointed. 'My favourite artist is Vincent Van Gogh,' she said hesitantly. 'And... I know everything about him.'

'Do you now?' He didn't sound...uninterested.

'Yes. I used to love going to art galleries and museums as a kid and looking at...beautiful things. And when I found a piece I particularly loved, I liked reading all about it and the person who made it.'

'Is that why you were able to explain Van Gogh's painting so eloquently?'

Bracing herself, Isla finally looked up from her

mug and met his gaze. He had that intent look on his face again, focused on her as if he'd never heard anything as fascinating as what she was telling him. It made something that had knotted tight and hard in her chest loosen slightly.

The most luminous thing in that gallery in that moment was you...

He'd told her that on their wedding night and she'd been so shocked by it. Because no one else had thought she was luminous when she talked about art. In fact, she never talked about it to anyone, because no one had ever been interested.

'It's one of my favourite paintings of his,' she said, still feeling shy. 'I love his use of colour.'

Orion's gaze didn't waver from hers. 'Tell me more.'

Her cheeks felt hot. 'You can't be interested.'

'Of course, I'm interested,' he said. 'I never say anything I don't mean.'

'It's nothing you won't already know.'

'But I don't,' he said gently. 'I know nothing about art or artists. The creative impulse baffles me, but I'd like to understand it. That's why I asked you to tell me about it.'

How could she say no to telling this supremely confident man something he didn't know? To help him understand something?

So she began to explain, hesitantly at first and then with more confidence, about Vincent Van Gogh's life and his early work. His mental health battles and his lack of acknowledgement from the art world. And Orion asked her more questions, about who else she liked, and so she told him about Millais and Rossetti, and the other Pre-Raphaelite artists, as well as Michelangelo and Titian, and then about some Greek sculptures she'd seen at the British Museum.

Orion listened the whole time, his attention never wandering, asking her questions and prompting her for more explanations. He appeared to be completely fascinated.

'And have you ever drawn anything?' he asked, after they'd both finished eating and were relaxing with the remainder of the coffee.

She shook her head. 'No. I don't think I have the talent.' And it wasn't that it hadn't occurred to her, it was just that drawing and art hadn't been appreciated by the foster families she'd been placed with. 'And it's not as if it's a viable career anyway.'

'How do you know if you haven't tried?' His mouth was curved in that half smile again, letting her know that it wasn't a challenge, more a question. And she realised with a sudden start that she hadn't felt unsettled or angry in his presence this time, not once. Only pleased to be talking with him about something she was passionate about.

'I wasn't adopted to be an artist.' She smiled back because she couldn't help herself. 'David wanted a CEO.'

And he didn't get one, did he?

The thought echoed uncomfortably in her head. Perhaps it was best if they changed the subject.

'Anyway,' she went on, 'that's my gift to you. Some boring art facts. If you want more, you'll have to wait for another day.'

Orion slowly sat back in his chair, giving her an enigmatic look. 'I suppose I can't argue with that. Though, for the record, I do want to know more and hearing you talk about it would definitely constitute a gift I would like to receive.'

The knot in her chest loosened further, something warm sitting there instead. She tried not to take any notice of it. 'Noted,' she said.

'Well,' he said. 'I liked my gift very much. Now it's time for yours.'

She tensed. If his gift was a kiss, she didn't know what she'd do. A gift couldn't be refused and she'd agreed to that. And if he kissed her, she'd… Well, she'd lose herself again, she just knew it. And that couldn't happen.

Orion smiled. 'How do you feel about a tour of an active volcano?'

He hadn't known what to expect when he'd given her his gift. He'd mentioned it as an activity he'd planned, but he hadn't known how she would take it. A gift couldn't be refused, yet if she'd really been afraid of the idea, he'd have thought of something else. Even her being afraid would have told him something about her.

But he suspected she wouldn't be. And he was pleased to find out he was right.

They started with an aerial tour in a helicopter flown by a local pilot, along with a geologist who gave them a rundown of the particular volcanic field they were visiting.

Given how much she'd enjoyed the painting in the gallery, he'd wondered if she'd like the colours of the landscape, the violent glow of lava and the pristine white of the snow. The deep mineral blue of the volcanic lakes and the black rock that surrounded them.

Then, after she'd talked to him at breakfast, about Van Gogh and the other artists she liked, about their histories and their inspirations and their methods, he *knew* she'd like the colours. And she did.

As they sat in the helicopter, flying around one of Iceland's most recent eruptions and he watched her stare out the window, there was no mistaking the glow of wonder that lit her face. The same glow he'd observed in the gallery.

Steam rose in clouds, thick moving lava glowing from underneath the black rock, and she watched it all with rapt, open-mouthed attention.

It made desire twist hard in his gut, along with a satisfaction at his own efforts to recreate that moment of luminous delight he'd seen that night at the gallery.

He still didn't understand why it affected him so intensely, though. It might have been a simple response to her beauty, because she was lovely when she looked like this. Then again, he'd seen plenty of lovely women before and he'd not felt this same, almost…visceral punch whenever he looked at her.

It was puzzling.

She'd intrigued him still further, though. He knew her background, that she'd been a foster kid like he had, except she'd been adopted, while no one had ever wanted him. He'd been too volatile as a kid, too hungry, too intense, and people seemed to sense that in him and shy away from it. He didn't blame them.

He was different now, of course, and he could see why David had chosen Isla to be his successor. She had a hunger too, though she probably wouldn't have said so, and the way she'd pursued the things that interested her struck a chord with him also. She wanted to understand things the way he did, researching all about those artists of hers and their lives. Trying to understand the art they made.

He'd thought that discovering one of her secrets might have dissipated some part of his fascination, but it didn't. If anything, it only made him even more intrigued.

The helicopter landed on a flat bit of rock and the geologist took Orion and Isla across the sharp ground to get a close-up view of a lava flow. Her face was rapt under her helmet—they both had on protective gear—as the geologist guided them across the sharp volcanic rocks, Isla peppering him with questions.

Once, she stumbled on the uneven ground and Orion instinctively slid an arm around her waist to steady her. She was so caught up in the tour she didn't seem to notice, leaning into him briefly before giving his arm a little pat, as if he was a dog, before pulling away to continue walking. And he found himself amused and aggravated in equal measure that she was so involved in the tour that she hadn't seemed to notice his touch.

You're a fool to let it matter to you this much. You've slept with her. What more do you need to know?

He couldn't have said. Only that sex was merely a part of his interest and that interest hadn't been satisfied yet. One thing he was sure of though, was that he couldn't move on from this obsession until he found the key, and so yes, it mattered. *She* mattered.

During the tour, he'd provided her with a camera since he thought she might want to take some better pictures than she could from her phone, and she hadn't protested. Not only had she asked the guide a million questions, but she'd spent just about every second taking photos of the rocks, the lava, the mountain and the snow, and once or twice, she'd even taken a couple of pictures of him.

He hadn't minded. If she wanted pictures of him, who was he to argue?

They spent a couple of hours exploring the mountain, and then a glacier, and in the helicopter afterwards, as they flew back to the lodge, she turned to him, her face alight, her blue eyes glowing. 'That was amazing! Honestly, I had no idea I'd enjoy getting that close to an active volcano. And all those colours… They were incredible!'

She wasn't self-contained now. The cork was out of that champagne bottle and she was fizzing everywhere, and not bothering to hide it. And he was seized by the almost uncontrollable urge to kiss her. He wanted to get a taste of her excitement and her joy, just a small taste, because it had been so long since he'd experienced anything like it, he couldn't remember what it felt like.

Have you ever *experienced anything like it?*

Possibly not. His life had had precious few moments of joy and wonder. Even his childhood had been lonely and isolated, the one bright spot being when he'd met Cleo. Except that had all gone to hell in a handcart and afterwards he'd decided he didn't need moments of joy. Satisfaction would do for him.

It would have satisfied him immensely to take a kiss from Isla, yet he held himself back. She'd been quite clear that she didn't want to sleep with him again, despite being still very attracted to him, and he found that for the second time in his life he didn't want to take something just because he could—and he could take that kiss. She wouldn't protest, he was sure of it.

Yet…he didn't want to. He wanted her to give a kiss to him of her own free will. Because she wanted to, because she wanted him, and not because he'd forced her into anything.

Especially after you forced her into marrying you.

Something uncomfortable shifted inside him. He'd told her that he hadn't regretted his threat to get her to marry him, but maybe he did. Maybe that hadn't been the correct course of action. Maybe that hadn't been the right opportunity to take.

He didn't like the feeling, just as he didn't like his own reluctance to take what he wanted from her. His ruthlessness, his edge, was what set him apart from others in the business world and he didn't want to lose it.

Except not enough to put his hand behind her head and draw her in for a kiss.

It was quite the conundrum.

'I thought you might like it,' he said instead, controlling himself firmly. 'From an artistic point of view.'

'Yes. I think I took about fifty million photos.' She grinned, her cheeks flushed with delight. 'Did you enjoy it too?'

It took him a moment to process the question, since he couldn't remember anyone ever asking him if he'd enjoyed anything. And it made the tight thing inside him shift yet again. Not only had she thought about him, she'd been interested enough to want to know if he'd shared her enjoyment. As if mattered to her.

For a second, he couldn't think. *Had* he enjoyed himself? Or had the entire day been more about his own satisfaction at putting that look on her face?

Yet deep in his frozen heart, like a small ray of

midwinter sun rising on a cold dawn, came the re-
alisation that, yes, he *had* enjoyed himself. He'd enjoyed watching her glitter and sparkle like sunlight
on snow, and he'd enjoyed her company. Her questions and her smile, and how she'd taken photos of
him as if she'd wanted to include him in her record
of this day. He'd also enjoyed sharing with her something that he found beautiful himself and having her
think so too.

Slowly he said, 'I did. Very much.'

She grinned. 'What was your favourite part?'

*When you stumbled and I caught you, and you
leaned against me. When you smiled and took my
photo. When you asked the geologist a question he
didn't know and he got a little irritated. When you
watched the lava flow, your whole face alight.*

The tight thing in his chest turned heavy, though
he had no idea why, so he ignored it. 'Oh,' he murmured. 'I couldn't pick just one.'

Isla laughed, the sound surprisingly husky, whispering over his skin like velvet. 'Really? Come on.
What do you like about volcanos?'

He thought about it for a moment and surprised
himself with the honesty of his answer. 'I think it's
very bracing to see nature's power close up. It's very
easy to only think of the world as a collection of cit-
ies full of humans, yet we live on a planet. And that
planet only allows us to be here on sufferance.'

Interest sharpened in her gaze. 'Yes, it's so easy
to forget we're sitting on top of a living planet, isn't

it? Is that why you chose to have a lodge here? For the landscape?'

Perhaps he should have bargained with her for the information, but he didn't even think about it. 'I have a few different houses in different places. But I come back to Iceland a lot. I like the isolation. The landscape is so wild and untamed and primal, and I like that too. Nature can't be tamed, all you can do is sit back and watch it with awe.' He smiled. 'It also has the gift of putting one's own problems into perspective.'

'Problems?' Amusement danced in her eyes. '*You* have problems? Please, what problems could the great and terrible Orion North have?'

The heaviness in his chest shifted again, gathering tighter. She was teasing him, with laughter in her blue eyes as she relaxed in the seat next to him, and she was just so…beautiful.

He almost couldn't look at her, the urge to grab her and pull her into his arms nearly overwhelming him. In fact, it shocked him how tenuous his control was. If he wasn't careful, the moment they landed, he really *would* grab her. He'd take her upstairs and rip her clothes off before she'd even had a chance to take a breath.

But he'd already decided he wasn't going to do that, and not just with a kiss either. When they slept together again, it would be because she wanted him, because she'd asked for it, because she'd given herself to him. It wouldn't be because he'd taken it.

So he forced away the tight feeling and gripped his control. 'Why, none, of course,' he said. 'Men like me don't have problems.'

The words must have come out less casual and more bitter than he'd intended, because she gave him a worried look. 'I'm sorry. I didn't mean to imply that you didn't.'

He was being ridiculous. The only problem he had was her. Everything else had been relegated to a past he no longer thought of.

So he gave her what he hoped was a reassuring smile and said, 'No need to apologise. My problems are purely of the business kind and aren't very interesting I'm afraid.'

But the worried crease between her brows didn't disappear. She opened her mouth to say something, then, clearly thinking better of it, shut it again. And as he watched, the excitement and the amusement died slowly out of her eyes, the glow in her cheeks fading.

You did that. You ruined it.

It made him feel suddenly as if he was back in the hallway at Cleo's place, watching Luke's family sing 'Happy Birthday', his heart burning with the knowledge that if he wanted to be part of Luke's life, no matter what he did, it would involve throwing a bomb in the middle of Luke's happy little family and blowing it to smithereens.

He hadn't been able to do it. He hadn't been able to rip his son's life apart, purely to heal his own pain.

You never bring happiness to people, do you?

That didn't matter. He didn't need to bring happiness to people. Happiness didn't interest him. The satisfaction he got from his business, the thrill of the chase and then the intellectual stimulation involved in stripping away the broken parts of a company to find the productive core was all he needed. That's where he got his enjoyment. He pruned away the deadwood so the tree could grow, cut out the scar tissue so the patient could get better.

That was all he needed from life. That was what made him content.

Happiness required you to care and he was done with caring.

He decided he was better off not saying anything after that and so he stayed quiet for the rest of the flight back to the lodge.

Once they were back, he helped Isla out of the helicopter and into the lodge, then he took himself off to his office, needing some distance.

Or at least he tried to.

They were in the entrance way, having divested themselves of their protective gear, and he was just on the point of striding down the hall, when Isla put a tentative hand on his arm.

He stopped dead, her light touch holding him as surely as iron chains. He had a T-shirt on and unfortunately it meant her skin was against his, burning like the flow of lava they'd seen not a couple of hours earlier.

'Did I…? Did I say something?' she asked hesitantly. 'In the helicopter? If I did, I'm sorry—'

'No.' The word was sharp but he couldn't moder-
ate his tone. 'You didn't. It was nothing.'

'But you—'

'Isla.' He turned around and looked down at her,
letting her see the heat in his eyes. It granted her
more power than she should have to reveal the extent of the effect she had on him, but she had to
know. He wouldn't break his vow over something as
meaningless as physical desire, however he wasn't
in the mood to make it harder for himself than it already was. 'I wouldn't touch me if I were you. Not
right now.'

Her gaze widened as it searched his, a flush of
colour in her cheeks. 'Orion, I—'

'I don't want to take it,' he interrupted yet again,
because he had to end this little scene right now and
with the truth. He didn't want to hurt her if he could
help it. 'I don't want to take you, do you understand?
I want you, but if sex happens between us again, it
will only be because you asked for it. I want it to be
a gift you give me. But if you keep touching me like
that, if you keep getting close to me, I might just
change my mind and take it anyway.'

Her lush mouth opened, but he didn't want to
stand here with her so close, discussing sex. He'd
said his piece and his control was already hanging
by a thread.

He needed to find it again.

So before she could say anything else, or worse, touch him again, he turned and strode off down the hallway.

CHAPTER SEVEN

ISLA DIDN'T SLEEP WELL that night and by the time dawn crept around, she was still tossing and turning in her bed.

She couldn't get the fierce gleam in Orion's eyes when he'd looked down at her in the hallway the night before out of her head. She'd only wanted to make sure that her teasing comment in the helicopter hadn't hurt him, which seemed ridiculous in retrospect since he seemed to be a man impervious to something as small as mere hurt.

The trip to the volcano had been a revelation, and she'd loved every second of it. The adrenaline rush of standing on the edge of a lava flow and listening to the geologist explain the workings of a volcano and how new rocks were made had been incredible. There had been so many things she'd wanted to know, so many colours to take in, the landscape around her in all its textures so fascinating.

It made such a change from the boardroom, and she'd got carried away in her excitement on the way back, thoughtlessly teasing Orion about his problems, because she'd never imagined a man like him would have any. Yet the sharpness of his response had brought her up short. She hadn't wanted to ruin the day by saying something careless, so in the hallway she'd only wanted to apologise.

Then he'd looked down at her and the heat in his eyes had locked the breath in her throat. As had the anger.

She hadn't realised he'd still wanted her, yet it was clear that he did. And badly. Except he wasn't going to take her. This time he wanted her to give herself to him.

Some part of her was thrilled at being such a test for his control, while another part was amazed that he was holding himself back from taking what he wanted.

She sighed and rolled onto her back, staring at the ceiling. The ferocious heat in his gaze, yet the rigid way he'd held himself in check had been an intoxicating combination. And far from making her not want to touch him, it made her want to keep touching him more. To push him, see how far she could take things before he broke…

'I want it to be a gift you give to me.'

Ah, but no, she couldn't push him. It wouldn't be right, not after he'd said that to her. Not now that he saw her as a gift to be given rather than a thing to take. It thrilled her down to the bone.

Twice she'd been chosen by people, and twice

they'd regretted that choice. The first time she'd been returned like a pet no one had wanted and the second time, well… She hadn't been returned by David yet, but she was still under review. Her performance had been lacking, she knew it.

You were stupid to expect more from him. You weren't adopted, you were hired.

It was true. David had never acted as though he was her father. Right from the first day she'd come home with him, he'd been emotionally distant. All he'd ever wanted from her were excellent marks at school and then honours at university, which she'd given him. She hadn't known any other way to earn his approval and she still didn't.

Why do you even want his approval?

She wasn't sure. Maybe it was simply that his approval was better than his disappointment, and she had never been able to bear that.

Not that she wanted to think of David. It was Orion and how she was going to deal with him today that mattered.

You didn't want to sleep with him again. You were very clear.

It was true, yet she couldn't deny how her body reacted to the thought of being in his arms again. The dragging ache between her thighs and the excitement that crowded in her throat. The way every muscle tightened with anticipation whenever he got close.

Yesterday, on the tour, she'd stumbled and he'd

slid an arm around her, anchoring her against his hard, powerful body. The shock of his warmth and the reassuring strength in his grip had unsettled her so much all she'd been able to do was pat his arm and step away as quickly as she could just to get her breath back.

Perhaps it was a reckless thing to contemplate, but would it be so very bad to offer herself to him? To give him the gift he wanted? Especially since she wanted him every bit as badly as he wanted her.

After all, she'd already had one night with him and nothing bad had happened afterwards. Her control over herself hadn't magically vanished just because she'd given in to passion. Was another night really such a risk?

Not finding any answers, eventually Isla hauled herself out of bed and got dressed. Then she found her camera from yesterday and went through the photos she'd taken, pleased with the shots. The stark, wild beauty of the Icelandic mountains and all that fire and ice set something vibrating deep inside her. And what had Orion told her in the helicopter on the way back? He'd spoken about nature's power and how it put things in perspective.

She'd liked his response. That he, a powerful man supremely in control of himself, could appreciate the untamed nature of the landscape. Not because he wanted to tame it, but because he wanted to get close to it, observe its majesty for himself.

Oh, he was interesting. She wanted to know more

of his thoughts on nature and she also wanted to know very much what problems nature put into perspective.

A photo of Orion suddenly popped up on her screen. He was standing on the black rocks, looking at her, a half smile curving his hard, beautiful mouth. His eyes were gleaming in the light from the lava flow and the intensity in his face stole her breath.

He looked fierce, as hard and sharp as the rocks he stood on. As powerful as the volcano that towered over them.

Such a beautiful man, though his wasn't a conventional beauty. It was something untamed and wild, as primitive as the landscape around him.

He'd given her such an amazing experience, and abruptly she wanted to do something equally amazing for him. Make his gift today one that would surprise and delight him as much as she'd been surprised and delighted the day before.

You know already what you're going to give him.

Isla put the camera down, her heart thudding. Oh, yes, she knew.

Another night, she decided. He'd wanted her to give him the gift of herself, so she would.

Orion was seated at the table by the time she'd finished dressing and come downstairs in search of breakfast. And once again his presence brought her up short, making her catch her breath.

He didn't smile at her this morning and he wasn't sitting with his usual casual posture. He looked tense, his face set in hard lines. 'Sit,' he ordered, his deep voice rough sounding. 'I want to give you today's present.'

Instinctive irritation at the sharp command prickled over her, but since he didn't look like he'd slept well, she swallowed her annoyance and did as she was told. They'd had such a lovely day yesterday and she didn't want to ruin the morning with an argument.

'You look like you slept as well as I did,' she observed as she sat down.

He ignored her. It looked like he'd been there a while. An empty plate with a knife and fork arranged neatly on it had been pushed away, a half-drunk cup of coffee at his elbow. 'My present to you today will be skating on the lake,' he said shortly.

He'd mentioned that as one of the excursions he'd planned a day or so ago, and then it had sounded fun. Looking at his hard expression now, she wasn't so certain.

'Are you sure?' She kept her voice very neutral. 'You don't seem as if you want to go anywhere let alone skating on the lake.'

'I'm sure.' He sat back in his chair, his expression still hard. A muscle flicked in his strong jaw, the amber of his eyes darkening, all the bright gold in them gone. He looked as intimidating and ruthless as he ever had.

Was that all because of her? Because he wanted her? Or were there other things at play here? Yesterday, in the helicopter, she'd made that casual comment about his problems and his expression had shuttered in much the same way. Why? Was it because he did have problems and he'd resented her mentioning them? Or was it for another reason? And why did it matter to her?

'Is this about yesterday?' she asked carefully. 'About what you told me in the hallway last night?'

'No,' he said coldly. 'Not everything is about you, Isla.'

Heat crept into her cheeks, a flicker of hurt going through her. She ignored it. 'That's not what I meant. I just wanted to know why you're sitting at the breakfast table looking like you want to break rocks with your teeth.'

'It's nothing.'

'Like it was nothing up in the helicopter yesterday?'

'Are you really that interested in my moods? I thought you were more interested in your favourite artists.' There was a hint of bitterness in the words, the way there had been yesterday, and he was radiating frustrated anger. She could feel it pushing at her from across the table like the heat from the lava flow the day before.

'Are you sulking because I wouldn't sleep with you?' she couldn't help asking, even though she knew confronting him was hardly likely to improve his mood. 'Is that what this is about?'

For a second he looked so fierce she thought he

was going to lose his temper, and it made her own anger rise, pulling at the chains she kept on it. She found herself staring at him almost hoping he would lose it, because she wanted to know what would happen if he did.

He was so controlled, so very in command of himself, and he would have seemed cold if not for that burning intensity in his eyes. There was fire at the heart of him, she realised suddenly. Fire that he couldn't let out for some reason.

Her heart raced and the strangest anticipation gripped her. And she was back on that volcanic field of yesterday once again, standing on the edge of a lava flow, looking up at the active volcano in terrified wonder as yet more lava flowed down its side.

Yet Orion didn't explode. Instead, he said. 'Give me my gift, Isla.'

It wasn't an answer, but it was most certainly a demand, and while it wasn't at all wise, Isla suddenly wanted very much to see what it would look like if Mt Orion North erupted.

'If you're going to sulk like a giant baby,' she said coolly. 'You'll have to wait for your gift. Skating first and then if you're very lucky I might give you something.'

Orion was in a foul temper. She was right, he hadn't slept well. He'd been up half the night, tortured by his desire for a woman he'd decided he wouldn't touch until she said he could. His vow infuriated him. The way it mattered to him infuriated him.

She infuriated him and he didn't know why.

Sex was nothing. He could deny himself till the cows came home and it had never bothered him before, and yet now he wanted her so badly it felt as if he couldn't breathe.

After hours of no sleep, he'd eventually had to get up and go into the lodge's gym to work out some of his frustration on the treadmill and then the rowing machine. A sauna had then eased the tension from his muscles, but of course, the moment she'd walked into the dining area, that tension had returned, even worse than it had the night before. And he was no closer to figuring out exactly why, hence the foul temper.

Then for her to stare at him coolly over the breakfast table and call him a giant baby... His temper roiled, pushing against his control.

She's not wrong. You are *sulking.*

He didn't appreciate that thought, not at all. Mainly because he knew it was correct. He also knew that if he didn't get hold of his temper, he'd end up ruining the skating on the lake that he'd planned for today and since he'd nearly ruined the volcano trip the day before, he didn't want to repeat his mistake.

Instead, he carefully and deliberately slid his chair back and slowly rose to his feet. 'Once you've had breakfast,' he said in the most neutral tones possible, 'come and meet me in the entrance hall and we can get geared up.'

Then without sparing her a glance, he left the dining area to prepare.

It was childish of him not to engage and definitely not to apologise, but he had to have some space to leash his hunger otherwise he was in danger of ruining this utterly.

A good half an hour later, Isla appeared, all cool and contained. Which of course made him want to crack her self-possession, put a dent in it somehow, ignite the fire that lit her up from within. But doing that when he was so on edge himself was a terrible idea, so he only handed her a thick white down jacket, a thick white scarf and hat and some gloves without a word.

Once they were both protected from the weather, he took both pairs of skates and led the way outside.

The morning was clear, the sky a deep, endless blue above them, the frigid air making white clouds of their warm breaths. There was a small wooden jetty that projected into the lake and they both sat down on it to put their skates on. He finished with his first and slid smoothly out onto the ice. He'd skated here many times and took pleasure in the solitude of the lake and the silence. He wondered if she too would appreciate that.

Turning, he watched as Isla gingerly put her skates onto the ice and slid out onto it, holding her hands out for balance. She looked adorable all wrapped up in the down jacket. Wisps of golden curls stuck out from under her hat, her scarf wrapped around her neck. She stayed where she was on the ice, still holding her hands out, as if she was afraid to move, and those deep blue eyes of hers were looking at him with trepidation.

'You haven't done this before, have you?' he asked.

She shook her head, and for some reason, the sharp edge of his mood eased.

He wanted her to enjoy this and she wouldn't if he stayed being angry. It was a gift, after all, and there should be pleasure in being given gifts. Or so he'd heard.

Orion skated over to her and took both her mittened hands in his. 'Just relax and keep your knees loose. I'm going to pull you along.' Keeping his grip firm, he began to slowly skate backwards, tugging her along with him.

She didn't fight him and soon the trepidation had gone from her eyes, and her cool self-possession along with it. She began to smile, her blue gaze sparkling as he went a little faster, giving her a few instructions on how to move, and he found himself smiling back, like a fool. But how could he not? She was irresistible. Glowing with that light he found so bewitching and again, he was the one who'd put it there.

He'd made her happy. Because that's what this was, wasn't it? It was happiness.

Don't worry, you'll ruin it soon. That's what you do. You destroy things.

His chest ached at the thought, but he pushed it away. He wanted to concentrate on this moment, not anything else.

'You're good at this,' she said, as they moved over the ice together.

'I've had a lot of practice.'

'What do you like about it?'

He moved in a slow gliding motion, drawing her along. 'It's very quiet and peaceful out on the ice. And sometimes it's as if you're the only person in creation.'

'You like being alone?'

'I'm always alone,' he heard himself say. Which was stupid. It revealed far too much about himself that he didn't want to share.

Yet a look of understanding shifted in her eyes. 'Me too,' she said. 'Since I was a kid.'

He slowed, the conversation more important than the skating all of a sudden. 'You were in the foster system, weren't you?'

'Yes. I was taken in by a family when I was around ten but…well, it didn't work out. And so I went into a home.'

He watched her face, drawn by the emotions shadowing her blue gaze. He too had been in a home, and he remembered the agony of wanting prospective adoptive parents to like him, to want him, to take him with them, to give him the family he'd always craved. Except they never had. But for her to have had a family only for it to be lost... He knew well what that agony was like.

'Why didn't it work out?' he asked and then, as a thought suddenly occurred to him, bringing with it a wave of protective anger so intense he could hardly breathe, he went on, 'Were they abusive?'

'No, nothing like that.' She glided forward as he moved back, managing to slide around a patch of rough ice. 'The couple already had a son and they wanted a girl. The son...didn't like me and would do things to get me into trouble. He was just a kid, like I was, but one day he scratched his dad's car and blamed it on me. And I'd taken the blame for months for various things, and that day I just...lost it.' She bit her lip, a shadow crossing her face. 'They didn't believe that it was their son, they just thought I was badly behaved and acting out, and so when I had a temper tantrum, that was the last straw. They decided that it would be best if they didn't adopt me after all.'

Orion was aware then of the strangest sensation in his chest. There was pain in her face and it was almost as if he could feel it too. Pain for her and what she'd experienced. Pain at the unfairness of it. Not to mention a violent anger at the carelessness of some people, who thought a child was a piece of furniture they could get rid of when it didn't fit their house.

He stopped on the ice and gently pulled her in close, his hands on her hips, holding her steady. 'And then what happened?'

She didn't pull away, only looked up at him. 'Then David adopted me. He liked my school marks and the reports from the people who ran the home. His late wife wanted him to adopt a girl and he needed an heir so he killed two birds with one stone.'

But this hurt her too and he could see that pain glittering in her eyes and he could feel it in his chest. He gripped her tighter. 'But that didn't work out either, did it?'

She took a small breath then glanced away. 'It wasn't…what I thought it was going to be.'

Orion put out a mittened hand to her jaw and gently urged her back to face him. 'Why not?' he asked, wanting to understand why this hurt her and perhaps why it also hurt him.

She sighed. 'I thought—hoped—that he might be a father to me. I thought he wanted a daughter, but… he didn't. He only wanted an heir, and he's been… disappointed in my performance.' She paused and then went on, 'He's been disappointed in his choice.'

A bright, fierce and protective anger turned over in Orion's gut. How dare David do that to her? How dare he find something as rare and precious as she was, and find it wanting?

He didn't question the intensity of the feeling, he only wanted to do something about the hurt in her eyes. 'David is a fool,' he said roughly. 'And if he regrets adopting you then he's even more of a fool than I thought he was.'

Isla's blue eyes turned dark. 'He's got reason,

Orion. I thought he was going to be my father, but after he brought me home, it was clear that he didn't think he was. I knew that it was my school marks he wanted, my potential as a future CEO, nothing else. He didn't actually want…me.'

The last word sounded as if she'd forced it out, and abruptly Orion was aware that he hated the thought of her thinking *she* was the problem. 'I stand corrected,' he growled. 'He *is* more of a fool than I thought he was.'

'It is me,' Isla said. 'I have a temper and I'm too volatile and I—'

'You're passionate,' Orion interrupted, not wanting to hear another word from her about all her shortcomings. Because they weren't shortcomings. None of them were. 'That's not a crime. You're smart, yes, but you're also interested, and you want to learn. You want to understand. In the boardroom all you need is more practice and better guidance. A mentor who will bolster your strengths not focus on your weaknesses.'

She stared at him and he was conscious that he was sounding far too vehement. But he didn't take any of it back. 'You really think so?' she asked, her voice husky. 'You really think there's hope for me?'

He couldn't stop himself then. He knew it was a bad idea, but he didn't want her hurt. He didn't want her believing she was somehow less because one man couldn't see the treasure that he'd found. He cupped her face in his hands, stared down into her eyes and let her see the belief in his. 'For months I've wondered what it is about you that has so fascinated me. Months, Isla. Ever since that night in the gallery. And I studied you, watched you, unable to think of anything but you. And I've decided it's not one thing. There are so many things about you that are interesting. Your fascinating mind and your passion. Your self-containment even when I can see there's a fire burning inside you. Your determination and your spine of steel. The way you matched wits with me and stood toe to toe with me, even as I was threatening your company.' Her eyes looking up into his were as bright as stars. 'The problem is *not* you. The problem was him. You wanted a father and that's what he should have been to you. A father, not a damn employer.'

She said nothing for a long moment. Then suddenly she reached up, took his face between her hands and pulled his mouth down on hers.

CHAPTER EIGHT

ORION'S LIPS WERE cool on hers, his body strong and powerful. It was stupid to kiss him on the ice when she could barely stand upright, but she couldn't help herself.

The fierce way he'd listed all her strengths, with the conviction gleaming in his wolf-gold gaze, as if he believed every single one of them had made her eyes prickle with tears.

No one had said those things to her before, not one person. No one had seen her temper as passion. Her father had only wanted her because of her school marks, but he hadn't told her she was smart or that she had a fascinating mind. Her determination had been detrimental to the board and her fire made her volatile, and her subsequent self-containment a blandness that was unacceptable.

They were all weaknesses not strengths.

No one had ever seen straight through to her heart and the secret fear that lay inside it that David had never wanted *her*, only her potential. That all the things that made her not CEO material, were also the reasons she'd never actually been his daughter.

Only Orion had seen those things. Only Orion, because he'd watched her, noticing things about her. Being interested in her. Months, he'd said. Months he'd been able to think of nothing but her. Ever since that night in the gallery.

She hadn't intended to tell him about her adoptive history, but when he'd said that he was always alone, she hadn't been able to stop herself. She knew what being alone felt like and she'd wanted him to know that too. Then he'd been so fierce when she'd told him about David, almost as if he was angry at David on her behalf and that's when her heart had felt painful. That's when she'd reached for him without thought.

He'd tensed and he didn't move, his mouth cool and smooth on hers.

He'd been so angry before and he wasn't now, but she could still taste the fire in him. The heat that only showed itself in his eyes. She wanted it to burn for her.

She put her arms around his neck, leaning into him and as she did so, she felt her skates begin to slide. But his hands were on her hips, steadying her. There were so many layers of clothes between them, the heat of his body tantalising her. She badly wanted all of those clothes gone.

Then his mouth lifted and she found herself looking up into eyes gone brilliant, flaming gold. 'What the hell was that for?' he demanded roughly.

A shiver worked its way down her spine and for some inane reason she felt like smiling. It was probably the taut look on his face, as if he was a junkie desperate for a fix and she was his drug of choice.

'That was my gift to you,' she said. 'I wanted to skate first and so we skated. And now I want to kiss you, if you'll let me.'

'If I'll let you?' he echoed, as if the words were foreign to him.

She loved the look on his face and the hunger in his eyes. 'You can't refuse a gift, Orion, remember? You have to take it.' She was teasing him and it was mean of her, but he'd threatened her into a marriage. He could stand a little teasing.

'Isla.' His hands tightened, bringing her hard up against his tall, powerful body.

'What?' She put her mittened palms flat to his chest, smiling up at him. 'I think I'm going to give you another gift too. That's allowed. We didn't say anything about not being able to give two gifts in one day.'

'Isla,' he said again, a warning this time.

She ignored it. 'I think I might want to give you another kiss. And this time in a place of my choosing.'

His gaze was nothing but gold now. *'Isla...'*

'You can't refuse.' Her knees felt unsteady, her heartbeat out of control. 'You have to take it.'

That muscle in the side of his jaw flexed, but he said nothing, the look in his eyes burning her to the ground.

'Where would you like it?' she murmured. 'Here or inside?'

'Is that all?' he demanded, rougher than the volcanic ground they'd walked over the day before. 'Is it just a kiss? Because you need to tell me.'

Isla decided to take pity on him. 'No,' she whispered. 'No, that's not all. You can have the rest of me too. If you want it.'

He went very still, searching her face as if to make sure that's what she was offering him. Then abruptly he picked her up in his arms.

Isla gave an undignified shriek. 'What are you doing?'

'Getting you back to the lodge.' He settled her against his chest. 'But we're doing this the fast way.'

Then they were gliding over the ice, the icy wind in her face, as he held her tight against his chest. He skated smoothly towards the jetty as if he'd been skating around with her in his arms for years, building up some speed. And when they reached it, he turned sharply on the edges of his skates, sending up a spray of ice as he stopped.

'Nice,' she murmured as he placed her on the side of the jetty and began undoing the laces of her skates himself. 'Are you trying to impress me?'

He looked up, his golden eyes brilliant. 'Perhaps. Is it working?'

'Perhaps,' she echoed, her heart now beating even faster, and smiled.

Orion dealt with their skates in record time, and then she was being pulled along the stone path back to the lodge, her mittened hands firmly in Orion's.

He got the front door open and once it had shut, he turned and pushed her up against it, holding her pressed to the wood by her hips, his head dipping to find her mouth.

'Kiss me,' he murmured against her lips. 'Give me your gift, Snow White.'

She could feel the tension in his body, the subtle vibration of a leashed predator desperate to be freed. It thrilled her to know how badly he wanted her and yet was holding back. And he must have wanted her *very* badly for him to shake like that.

He wanted his gift and so she gave it to him.

She tilted her head back and met his mouth, pressing her lips to his, gentle and soft. She felt the shudder that went through him and braced herself for the explosion, yet it didn't come. He remained still, as if waiting for more.

So she gave him more, tracing his mouth with her tongue, nipping at his bottom lip. And then when his lips parted, allowing her entry, she tasted him deeper, loving how he let her explore him, chasing his delicious flavour, because the more she had, the more she wanted.

Her hands were pressed to the hard plane of his chest and she arched into him, the throb between her thighs becoming demanding. Then the leash he had on himself snapped.

Orion lifted his head, his eyes gleaming with hunger. He pulled her mittens off, then her hat and her scarf. Then he proceeded to rip off the rest of her clothes, discarding them along with her boots in a heap on the floor.

He dealt with his own in seconds flat and then she was being taken down to the floor in the hallway, a soft rug beneath her, Orion's powerful body over her. She put her hands to his shoulders and stroked him, loving the feel of his hot skin, and the strong muscles that shifted and flexed beneath it. His mouth was on hers, the kiss getting deeper, hotter, and she returned it, as feverish and needy as he was.

He slid one hand between her thighs, finding the slick heat there and stroking her, making her gasp and shake, shifting beneath him because she wanted more, so much more. But he didn't give it to her.

Instead, he rolled over and she found herself sitting astride him. He had a condom in his hand. 'Put it on me,' he ordered, his voice gravelly and raw, his eyes blazing with demand. 'Now, Snow White.'

Her hands shook as she ripped open the packet and not because she was afraid. She was hungry too and the look in his eyes was making it difficult to think. He was desperate for her and she loved it. She wanted the explosion. She wanted the volcano he was to erupt.

She rolled on the condom and his hand came

down over hers, holding her fingers tight around him, showing her how to stroke him. Her breath hitched as she followed his movements, watching as the gold in his eyes burned bright.

'Come here,' he growled at last. 'Put me inside you.'

So she did, lifting herself up and then sliding down onto him, his hands on her hips to guide her, feeling the delicious burn of her sex stretching around his, holding him tight.

He made a growling sound deep in his throat, and then he was showing her how to move and what rhythm gave them both the most pleasure. She fell into it naturally, easily, as if they'd been lovers for years and knew each other's bodies as well as their own.

She couldn't look away from his beautiful face, set in lines of taut hunger, gazing at her as if he wanted to eat her alive. And as the pleasure climbed higher, becoming more intense, more demanding, she didn't know what she'd been afraid of.

This was like skating, like flying. Like standing on the edge of a volcano with the wild glory of nature all around her. There was no stopping it. No controlling it. She wasn't ice and neither was he. They were both fire and they were letting that fire burn.

She moved faster, harder and then he rolled again, taking her beneath him and everything became hotter and more desperate. He grabbed her behind the knee and pulled her leg up around his waist, sliding deeper inside her and she couldn't breathe for the pleasure.

His mouth covered hers and he was inside her, around her. All she could taste was the delicious flavour of him and the dark spice of his scent surrounded her, and she couldn't think of anywhere she wanted to be right now but here, under him.

It was agony. It was ecstasy. And then suddenly it was a release that blinded her.

She screamed against his shoulder as the pleasure overwhelmed her, and dimly she heard him call her name as he followed her into the flames.

She was persuasive, his snow maiden. After the wild sex in the hallway, she tried to convince him that a soak in this fabled hot pool of his was just what she needed. But he'd been saving that gift and anyway, he wanted her somewhere warm and soft so he could have her whenever he wanted her. Which was all the time.

So he took her upstairs to the bedroom for a little while and when they were both satisfied for the moment, he ran a bath in the huge white marble tub in his bathroom. He got in with her and they both lay there in companionable silence, watching the snowy landscape out the window.

But of course, she was wet and slippery and one thing led to another which led them back to bed again.

He couldn't seem to get enough of her.

That night he explored her as thoroughly as he could and then it was her turn to explore him, which he liked a great deal. Yet the puzzling thing was that instead of his hunger getting less, it only seemed to deepen still further. She'd finally given him the gift of her body and he'd thought that once he'd had her again, he wouldn't be so hungry. But he was. He didn't understand it.

That might have concerned him if he hadn't known that he had another ten days of Christmas gift giving, which meant a lot of time to fully comprehend what was going on with her, and so he decided that holding back now wasn't an option. Clearly to get to the bottom of his fascination, he was going to have to go all in.

The next morning, he woke with her in his arms, nestled against him, her golden curls spread across his chest, and the pleasure that gave him was indescribable. He'd never felt anything like it. It was satisfaction and desire and a savage need to hold her close and never let her go in order to keep her safe.

The intensity of it set off some alarm bells, but since he wasn't holding back, he ignored the disquiet. Instead, he woke her with soft kisses that soon turned into hotter kisses and then a blazing desire that took at least an hour to fully satisfy.

Afterwards, she lay with her head on his chest, idly tracing circles on his skin, her lush mouth, still red from his kisses, curving in a self-satisfied smile that made him want to growl with pleasure.

'Your body is mine,' he said, feeling unaccountably possessive. 'You made it a gift to me and now I'm keeping it for the next ten days.'

She arched one golden brow, the blue of her eyes hot as a midsummer day. 'Is that a fact?'

'It is,' he said definitively. 'There will be no argument.'

'Bossy man.' She gave him a lazy smile. 'But I suppose I'll allow it.' She folded her hands on his chest. 'So, it's morning again and I don't have a gift.'

Idly, he took one of her curls between his fingers and tugged gently. 'Impatient woman. What about mine?'

Colour washed through her cheeks and her lashes lowered. 'I'm not sure I have anything else to give you. I already told you my secret.'

'That's not the only secret you have, I'm sure.'

She sighed. 'There really isn't that much to me, I'm afraid.'

'I don't believe that for a second.' He wound the soft silkiness of her curl around his finger. 'There's so much I don't know about you. For example, what's your favourite colour? And your favourite food? Your favourite book?'

She gave him a look from beneath her lashes. 'Those aren't secrets.'

'They're still gifts.' He held her gaze. 'Everything about you is a gift.'

The pink in her cheeks deepened. 'You're a shameless flatterer.'

'Come on.' He tugged insistently on her curl again. 'Tell me something about you that I don't know.'

'Well, okay.' She bit her lip, clearly thinking. Then she said, 'I actually hate Christmas.'

He couldn't help smiling at that. 'The Christmas CEO who hates Christmas? Sounds like the beginnings of a romantic comedy.'

'It's true,' she protested, smiling too. 'I hate it. But not because it's David's business. It's more because I don't think I've ever had a proper Christmas the way other people have it.'

He hadn't ever had a proper Christmas either. He'd never known his parents and the foster parents he'd been placed with had all been various shades of uninterested, distracted and/or outright abusive. There had never been Christmas trees in his childhood. Never been presents either. Not for Christmas and none at all for his birthday, if anyone bothered to remember it. In fact, his childhood had been nothing but a hard slog.

Until he'd met Cleo. He'd been working in a garage helping out as a mechanic's assistant when her father had brought his expensive Porsche in for repair. Cleo had been with him and she'd been beautiful, so soft and delicate; he'd never seen anything like her. They'd got talking and she'd been as taken with him as he with her and they'd swapped numbers. Then they'd meet up in secret, since Cleo wasn't allowed out at night. It had turned physical very quickly and then, because they were sixteen and hadn't been careful, she'd fallen pregnant. Then everything had gone to hell.

In her and their child he'd seen the family he'd never had and so he was desperate to hold on to them both. He was earning money in the garage. He was sure he could support them. But Cleo's parents had found out about the pregnancy and had forbidden him to see her, though that hadn't stopped him from trying. He'd turned up on their doorstep one night, insisting on seeing her and generally making a pest of himself. Even threats to call the police hadn't worked. So Cleo herself had at last come to the door and she'd looked him in the eye, telling him that he needed to leave. That there was no future for them. She didn't love him, she didn't want him and frankly it was best for their baby if he wasn't in their lives.

Back then he'd thought her father had turned her against him, so full of uncontrollable teenaged fury, he'd returned with a baseball bat and had taken it to her father's Porsche, smashing the headlights and the front panels, and the windscreen.

He'd been stupid. Her father had called the police, he'd been charged, and a non-molestation order had been issued, forbidding him from contacting Cleo or her family. And he'd lost his son. He probably would have lost him anyway, but that one moment of rage had guaranteed it.

So he'd decided to fight, to work hard, accumulate as much money and power as he could, since if you were rich and powerful you could do whatever you wanted. And then he'd get his son back.

It hadn't worked out that way, but he'd never regretted the decision he'd made to leave Luke where he was. He couldn't find happiness for himself, but he could give it to his son and so he had.

That had been the last time he'd ever given anyone anything. Until Isla.

'What made it different?' he asked, watching her pretty face.

'We didn't have a Christmas tree,' she said. 'Or presents. Instead we'd donate our time to various charities, so I did a lot of volunteering in homeless shelters or children's charities. I didn't mind that, and I didn't mind not receiving presents. It wasn't about getting "things". It was just... Christmas is about spending time with your family, but David never spent any time with me.' Her finger drew another small circle on his chest, her attention on it. 'That's what I always wanted for Christmas. Just some time with him where we felt like a family. But he never gave it. I kept thinking that maybe if I'd been different somehow, he might have treated me like a daughter, but...he never did.' She gave a faintly bitter laugh. 'I was never allowed to call him Dad, for example. He adopted me legally, but we weren't a family.'

Orion could hear the hurt in her voice and it made him want to growl. And in fact, the more he heard about David the more he wanted to fly all the way to the UK and give the man the sharp edge of his tongue. Or perhaps a punch in the face. He didn't know what David had been thinking to adopt a young girl and then deprive her of the one thing she wanted most. It was cruel and thoughtless.

He dropped her curl and touched her cheek instead, stroking her silky skin. 'Is that what you wanted?' he asked softly. 'A family?'

She leaned into his touch, the unconscious movement making his chest tighten. 'Yes. That's why I was going to marry Gianni. David said that it was important that the future CEO have a family since Kendricks' is a family company, and that it was time I started mine. He wanted me to marry someone within the company too, and he thought Gianni and I would be a good fit.'

The subject of Gianni made Orion want to growl yet again. 'You didn't want him,' he said, unable to keep the possessive note from his voice.

Isla's blue gaze looked up and met his. 'No. You were right, I didn't. I didn't love him either. But I... hoped that maybe one day I would.'

He could see the truth in her eyes. She *had* wanted that.

'A family is important to you?' He didn't know why the words felt as if they were echoing hollowly inside him.

She nodded. 'I never had one of my own, Orion. I was given the taste of one. In fact, I had the taste of one twice, but... The first one didn't work out and with David… Well, that wasn't even a family. I was an employee, not a daughter.'

She deserves one, too, especially after David essentially sold her to you. And you can't give it to her.

His chest felt unaccountably tight. He could see that now, how little Kendrick had cared for the daughter he'd adopted, for the person that she was. How he wanted an ideal to head his company, someone exactly like himself, not a living breathing woman with thoughts and feelings and desires of her own.

And you were complicit in that.

He didn't like that thought. He didn't like how regretful and vaguely ashamed of himself it made him feel. It didn't help knowing he'd never give anyone a family let alone her either. And not because he couldn't, but because he didn't want to. He'd had a partner and a child once, and he'd wanted to keep both of them more than he'd wanted his next breath.

But Cleo and his child had been taken from him. Cleo by her parents and then by her own choice, and his child along with her.

He'd had his taste of a family and when he'd lost it, it had nearly broken him. He didn't want to do it again, not for anyone.

'You'll find a family of your own one day, Snow White,' he said. 'Of that I have no doubt. In the meantime, I don't see why *we* can't have a proper Christmas.'

Emotions flickered in her blue gaze, so many

and so fast he couldn't untangle them all. But then the sharp glitter of pain faded and her mouth softened. 'I'd like that. Did you ever have one? A proper Christmas, I mean?'

'No. I grew up in the foster system, like you did, and the homes I was placed in never seemed to celebrate it.'

Interest lit her eyes. 'Oh? What happened to your parents?'

There was no reason not to tell her. 'I never knew them. They were itinerant workers, traveling around Europe, and I think I was born somewhere in the Mediterranean, though no one quite knows for certain since I never had a birth certificate. They came to the UK eventually—don't ask me how—and were found one morning dead in a tent in a campsite. Overdose, I was told later. Anyway, someone heard me crying and so I was rescued and put into care.'

Her brow creased with sympathy. 'I was the child of a single mum. She died when I was four and she had no family so I was put into care too.' She stared at him as if he was the most interesting thing she'd ever seen in her life. 'I had no idea you had the same experience.'

He liked the way she looked at him. It was addictive as hell. 'My background isn't a secret. There are numerous bios floating around on the internet. It wasn't pleasant, but I got through it.'

'I want to hear all about it.' She pressed her mouth

to his chest and gave him a kiss. 'But first I want my present.'

He smiled. 'Not only impatient but demanding too. Say please and I might tell you what it is.'

Excitement sparkled in her gaze. 'Please tell me it's the hot pool.'

'I couldn't possibly say.'

'Orion.' She shifted, sliding the rest of her body on top of his, pressing her delectable curves against him. 'Tell me.'

He was getting hard again, hunger turning his blood hot. He ran a hand down her back and squeezed the soft flesh of her bottom, making her gasp. 'Say please.'

'Please,' she murmured breathlessly. 'Tell me about my present, *please*.'

He laughed and told her. 'Yes, the hot pool. Tonight.'

CHAPTER NINE

THE HOT POOL turned out to be in a small hidden gorge just behind the lodge. The water was a bright mineral blue and steam rose from it in clouds. A wooden path led to the pool from the lodge, which then gave on to a flat area flagged in stone with some stone steps that led down into the water. A small wooden changing cabin stood nearby, well equipped with thick, fluffy towels, though they didn't need the cabin and Isla didn't need her bikini either since they were swimming naked.

Orion was already in the water by the time Isla had finished stripping off, and he stood in the middle of the pool, by the stone steps, his hand outstretched to help her down. She was freezing, the stone beneath her bare feet icy, and as she took his hand and went quickly down into the hot water, she gasped a little at the shock of it. It felt so warm and silky sliding over her skin after the frigid air, making her shiver.

The pool was wonderfully deep and she followed Orion into the deeper water, getting her shoulders under and sighing in pleasure as the heat stole away the remaining cold.

There was something magical about being submerged in warm water while snow drifted in the air.

The gorge itself was lit with small lights powered by solar batteries, the illumination enough to see the path and the edge of the pool, but not enough to obscure the glittering black bowl of the night sky upturned above them.

Orion was behind her, his powerful arms circling her as she leaned back against him, looking up at the stars. He'd promised her the northern lights tonight and she was excited to see them. In fact, she'd been excited about everything the past couple of days and she couldn't remember the last time she'd felt that.

She hadn't regretted her decision to sleep with him again, not for a single moment. And when he'd laid claim to her body that morning, she'd decided that well, he could have it. She hadn't thought what would happen the next day when she'd given herself to him in the hallway the day before, and that he wanted to keep her in his bed for the whole of the next ten days was okay by her. More than okay.

She still felt bad that her gifts to him weren't nearly as wonderful as his were. He'd said that he wanted to know more about her, but she was running out of interesting things to tell him. Were her favourite colour and food really all that interesting? He'd been amused by her Christmas confession, which had pleased her, and then he'd been so understanding when she'd told him why. And when he'd told her about his own childhood, and how similar it had been to hers, she'd felt…almost amazed. She'd met very few people who'd had similar experiences and to find that he'd been in the foster system too… Well, it had felt as if a bond had been created between them.

She felt vaguely ashamed of herself that she hadn't known. Then again, she hadn't liked him for a long time and had told herself she didn't want to know anything about him. Perhaps if she'd known about his childhood, she might have felt differently.

Not that it mattered. She felt differently about him now. In fact, she thought she might like him now. She definitely liked the way he touched her, the bonfire they created between them when they were in bed together. And she liked how he listened to her, looking at her as if every word that came out of her mouth was of intense interest to him. She liked how he teased her and how there was affection and warmth in his cold, deep voice whenever he did so. And she liked how he responded when she teased him, the amber of his eyes glinting with a wickedness that only made her want to tease him even more.

In fact, the only shadow on the day had been that morning when they were in bed together and he'd said, *'You'll find a family of your own one day, Snow White.'*

She didn't know why that made a kind of hollowness gather in her chest. Because she *would* find a family of her own one day. A family that was hers, that she got to keep. Who wouldn't send her away or be disappointed because she wasn't what they wanted.

It wouldn't be with Orion, naturally. It would be with someone who wanted the same things she did. Who would be good for the company, of course, and who would love to have children, because she wanted children.

She didn't have to be in love with him. Love had been a scarce commodity in her own life—in fact, she didn't know if anyone had ever loved her, apart from her mother—but she'd managed to survive without it so far. And if it took time for love to develop between her and her chosen partner, then she was fine to wait for it.

You could fall in love with Orion.

The thought streaked through her brain like a comet streaking through the night sky, a brief burst of glowing light that she quickly shoved away. No, she wasn't going to fall in love with Orion. Absolutely not. He didn't love her and while that wasn't necessary, she did want someone who'd stick around for the duration. And he definitely wouldn't. He'd already told her that she was only here so he could get to the bottom of his fascination with her and then once he had, he'd move on.

Plus, he'd said that he hoped she'd find her family one day, obviously implying that it wouldn't be with him. Which was fine. Absolutely fine. She didn't want to be with someone who didn't want her and didn't want what she wanted.

Their marriage had to stand for a year, according to his promise, but after that she'd be free to find someone else. She didn't know why that thought made her throat close up.

Orion shifted her head so it rested on his shoulder and then pointed out a few of the major constellations, murmuring softly in her ear.

'Where's your belt?' she said, hoping to make him laugh.

And he did, a soft rumble in her ear. 'Very funny.'

'I bet you get that a lot.'

'Not as much as you might think.' His hands drifted over her beneath the water, undemanding and gentle.

The sky was black and deep above them, the stars glittering pinpricks of light.

Except she couldn't concentrate on the sky, not when she was resting against his hot skin and his hands were on her, making her shiver and ache, making her long for something she couldn't name.

'Are you going to tell me any secrets?' she asked him idly. 'Or do I only get a fun itinerary of excursions?'

His hands stroked down her thighs. 'Do you want secrets from me?'

She wasn't sure why she was asking him about it. Probably because all her gifts to him seemed lame in comparison with volcano tours, skating and hot pools. Plus, he said he was fascinated with her and wanted to know her, but she wanted to know about him too. And he hadn't told her much about himself.

'I like what you've given me so far, don't get me wrong,' she said. 'I've loved the volcano and the skating, and this pool is magical, but... You know quite a lot about me, but I don't know anything about you apart from the fact that you were in the foster system.'

His hands slid up over her stomach and cupped her breasts. 'I wasn't aware you were interested in more than excursions.'

There was no heat in the words and yet she could sense a sudden tension in him. 'Perhaps I am.' She tried to sound as if she didn't care one way or the other. 'Perhaps I'd like to hear a couple of secrets. I can't be the only one to give up mine.'

He didn't say anything for a long moment. 'That would constitute an extra present.'

'I know, but I gave you an extra one yesterday,' she pointed out. 'A kiss *and* me.'

His thumbs circled her nipples lazily. 'Are you sure you wouldn't rather have something else?'

He was trying to distract her. Which meant that he didn't want to tell her. So, did that mean he did have secrets? And did that also mean that they were painful? If his childhood hadn't been easy then his life couldn't have been, so maybe they were.

'I might,' she allowed, since she was starting to feel hot and it wasn't just the water in the pool. 'But I'd rather have a secret first.'

For a long moment he was silent. Then his hands dropped from her breasts and he slid an arm around her waist, bringing her over to the side of the pool where there was a stone seat beneath the water.

He sat her down on it and then sat beside her, tilting his head back as he stared up at the sky. 'When I was sixteen I fell in love, and she fell pregnant unexpectedly. She came from a wealthy family, and I was just a sixteen-year-old foster kid working in a garage, and her family didn't approve. When they found out about the pregnancy, they stopped me from seeing her, and when our son was born, they stopped me from seeing him too.'

Isla went very still. His voice was smooth and even, betraying no hint of his feelings. He said the words as if they'd happened a long, long time ago and to someone else.

'I was furious, of course. When Cleo's father told me I couldn't see my son, that I wasn't even named on his birth certificate, I took a baseball bat from home and smashed up his car with it. That naturally enough earned me a police warning and a non-molestation order.'

The breath went out of her, a soundless sigh of shock. Again, his face betrayed nothing but casual interest as he stared at the sky. But the fact that he was searching it so intently told her everything she needed to know.

This was painful for him. Terribly, exquisitely painful.

'I swore that I'd get him back at some point,'

Orion went on. 'When I had enough money and power, and about ten years ago, that's exactly what I did. Or at least that's what I intended to do.'

Isla realised she'd gone tense in the water, staring at him fascinated. 'What happened?' she asked, because something had. She hadn't heard anything about him having a child.

'Oh, I decided that I'd leave him with his family,' Orion said casually. 'I walked in during his birthday party and he was surrounded by his family, and he was so…happy.' For the first time Isla heard a hint of roughness in his voice. 'I couldn't take him away from that. He didn't know me. He didn't even know I existed. And I couldn't bring myself to take a ten-year-old boy away from the only family he'd ever known. So I turned around and walked out.'

There was a lump in Isla's throat, and it was painful. She swallowed, her heart aching. A few days ago she wouldn't have believed him. He was a man who took what he wanted, when he wanted it—that's what he'd told her. Yet he hadn't taken back his own child. He'd seen that his son was happy and he'd put his child's happiness before his own.

What must it have been like for him to come into that party and see his son surrounded by people who loved him? Seeing him happy? And knowingly giving that up for himself…

Isla stared at Orion's rough, handsome profile as he looked up into the sky. At the hard lines of his face. 'I'm sorry,' she said thickly. 'That must have been—'

'Good,' he said, cutting her off. 'It was good. And satisfying to know he was loved and he was happy.' His hard mouth curved in a smile that had nothing of amusement in it. 'The gift of my absence was the only thing I could give him in that moment and so that's what I gave him.'

She could hear the roughness in his voice again, so very slight and not at all noticeable if she hadn't been listening for it. But she had been listening for it.

The gift of his absence...

God, how painful that must have been for him. He was an intense man, a passionate man, and there was fire in him deep down. She'd seen it burn. He must have wanted his child badly and to have to give that child up. To have that child never even know he existed...

Her heart twisted painfully and tears prickled behind her eyes. But it wasn't her sadness to bear, it was his, so she forced it away. 'Have you ever tried to meet him since?' she asked. 'Or has he ever tried to contact you?'

Orion shook his head. 'I decided it would be easier for all concerned if I just pretended he didn't exist for me the way I didn't exist for him. So no, I haven't contacted him nor has he contacted me. I don't know where he is or what he's doing and it's better that way.'

Isla looked away, blinking fiercely against the insistent tears. 'How could they take him away from you?' she couldn't help asking, her heart burning at the unfairness of it. 'How could they not even acknowledge you?'

He shrugged. 'I was just some poor kid who'd impregnated their daughter. And Cleo… She was so young and she was scared. I told her I'd look after her, but I wouldn't have been able to. I was sixteen. I had no qualifications and my job was part-time and paid a pittance. I couldn't have looked after a partner and a child, no matter how badly I wanted to at the time.'

'That wasn't fair,' she said, knowing she shouldn't keep pressing the issue, but unable to stop herself. 'They should have allowed you contact at least.'

Orion finally glanced at her, amber eyes dark. 'After I'd taken a baseball bat to the family car? I don't think so. And I don't blame them for it either. I was young and stupid and full of rage, and I wouldn't have allowed contact with me either.'

He's not angry, so why are you? It's not your trauma.

Except he was angry, she was sure of it. He was so rigidly controlled, keeping all the fire inside him locked down, and there had to be a reason for that. Was it to do with his son? Was it to do with the fury he must still feel and the pain that had to be there? Fury and pain that had nowhere to go and so he simply locked them both away?

She stared into his eyes and yes, she could see that wolf gold gleaming. He felt the pain of having a child he could never acknowledge, and the rage of having that child taken from him. Then the agony of knowing he could never see that child again, because that was what was best for the child.

I gave him the gift of my absence...

No one would ever know what he'd sacrificed. No one except her.

Isla didn't know what to say. She didn't have a child, but she knew what it was like to have the family she'd once longed for denied, and she knew how painful that was.

So she turned to him, shifting on the stone seat so she was sitting in his lap, facing him. Then she took his face between her hands and kissed him.

Isla's mouth was soft and hot and he could taste salt on her lips. They were tears, tears for him.

He wanted to tell her that she didn't need to cry for him, that what had happened with Luke was all in the past. That he was done with it now and had come to terms with it. But there was something burning inside him, the rage and the pain that had never dissipated despite the years and all the assurances he'd made to himself. The love for a son he would never know and who would never know him.

It enraged him to feel any of those things. He'd thought he'd cut them out of his heart, but it seemed they were still there, and they ached, they burned.

He shouldn't have told her about Luke. He should never have said anything, but she'd wanted a secret from him and that was the only secret he had. He'd thought he should tell her anyway, after that conversation they'd had in bed that morning, and how she'd mentioned wanting a family. Whether she felt anything for him at all beyond desire or not, she should know at least that she couldn't look to him for that family, and here was the one reason why.

It should have been easy to tell her. It shouldn't have hurt. Yet when he'd turned to her and found her watching him, anger burning in her blue eyes, he could feel the pain ache inside him.

She's right. It wasn't fair.

Perhaps it wasn't, but there was nothing to be done about it now. He'd made his decision back in that Chelsea townhouse and if he had to make that decision again, he'd make the same one. But he didn't want her to hurt for it. That wasn't why he'd told her.

He lifted his hands and pulled her's away from him, raising his head. She was staring at him, the expression on her face fierce with sorrow and anger.

'Don't,' he said. 'Don't be sad for me. It was the only decision I could have made.'

'I know. Of course you wouldn't have wanted to take him away from his family. But *you're* his family too. You know that, don't you?'

Something shifted inside him, the ache a grief that never went away. He ignored it. 'I'm not his father, Isla,' he said. 'I didn't bring him up. I haven't been in his life. I'm nothing but a stranger to him.'

'You *are* his father. His biological father.' Her eyes glinted deep sapphire in the night. 'He'll want to know where he came from and what happened to you and I know that, because I never knew my biological father myself. He wasn't on my birth certificate. I've got nothing and I wish I could have had something.'

She was warm and slippery and silky in his lap and there were many other things they could be doing right now other than talking about a past that was dead and gone.

'Let it go.' He put his hands on her hips, holding her carefully. 'I have.'

'No, you haven't.' She was still staring fiercely at him. 'You're angry, Orion. I can see it in your eyes. And it hurts you, doesn't it?'

He could feel the heat of it in his chest, the sharp edges of a fire that had never burned itself out. She saw too much, his snow maiden.

'I made my choice,' he said flatly. 'I let him go. And it's easier if he stays gone.'

'Easier for who? For him or for you?'

Anger gathered in his gut and he couldn't help responding to it. 'This is none of your business, Isla, and I didn't ask for your input.'

Yet her jaw was tense and she didn't look away. 'He'll be twenty now. He'll be an adult. He'll be able to make decisions for himself about whether he finds out who is father is.'

'Yes, well, and he hasn't.' The words came out of him with such bitterness he could hardly believe he'd said them.

Isla's gaze flared, a deep sympathy in it that caught at the edges of his emotions as if they were still raw and new, making them hurt. 'Oh, Orion,' she said softly.

Abruptly he couldn't bear to be there with her any longer. He didn't want her looking at him like that, he didn't want her digging at the wound in his heart he'd thought long healed. He'd come to terms with the fact that he didn't have his son in his life and he'd chosen that himself. The fact that Luke hadn't contacted him was neither here nor there, and he wasn't upset about it. At all.

He tightened his grip on her hips, wanting to put her off his lap, but her arms were around his neck all of a sudden, and her cheek was against his shoulder, and he could feel the soft heat between her thighs pressing against him.

'I'm sorry,' she whispered. 'I don't mean to push you. I don't want to make it worse. It's just…not fair. You're a good man and you didn't deserve for him to be taken away from you.'

His throat was tight for a second and he couldn't move, couldn't breathe. 'I was angry,' he heard himself say. 'I smashed up that car. No child deserves a violent, angry father.'

'You were a sixteen-year-old boy.' Isla turned her head and kissed his chest, her lips warm against his skin. 'A boy who'd been through the foster system. It's not as if you had the emotional maturity to know what you were doing. And they didn't give you a chance. That's on them, not you.'

Orion shut his eyes. He didn't know why he was still sitting there, listening to her, when he'd been about to get up and leave. He wanted distance, didn't he? He didn't want to keep talking, not about Luke. He'd made the right decision all those years ago, he had.

'I couldn't go back,' he said hoarsely. 'I knew I wouldn't be welcome and besides, I couldn't do anything. Cleo's father had money and contacts and I was...nothing. But I swore that one day, when I had money and power, I'd come back for him. Except I couldn't take him then either.'

Isla pressed another kiss to his chest. 'You put your child first. That's what a good father does.'

He wasn't gripping her now, his hands still on her thighs, the ache in his heart sharp and jagged. 'If I was a good father, I'd have fought for him more.' He shouldn't be telling her this and yet he couldn't seem to stop. 'If I was a good father, I wouldn't have let him go.'

'You *didn't* let him go.' Isla lifted her head, her blue gaze burning. 'You couldn't stop them, because you were too young. And by the time you were old enough to get him, you *couldn't*. Not without destroying his life.'

He knew that was only the truth and yet... Why did it feel as if he could have done things differently?

As if he'd let his son slip through his fingers. As if he hadn't fought for him at all.

And you're doing the same thing now.

The thought slid through him, sharp and insidious, and abruptly he was sick of talking.

He shifted one hand to her hip and gripped it, before sliding his fingers up her inner thigh. 'I'm tired of talking about this,' he said roughly. 'I'd prefer to do something else.'

But Isla ignored him. 'Why haven't you looked for him?'

The question felt like the edge of a knife against his skin. 'Didn't you hear me?' he snapped. 'This subject is closed.' It was a warning and he'd intended it to be.

Yet again, she just ignored him, her gaze searching. 'What are you afraid of?'

The knife slid into him, so sharp he barely felt the cut. But he certainly felt the pain, bright and hot.

You know what you're afraid of. That he'll blame you. That he'll tell you that you didn't fight hard enough. That you didn't want him enough. That he needed you and you weren't there for him.

The water was warm, but he felt the ice in his gut, sharp as a sliver of glass.

He needed distance. He needed to get away from Isla and her interrogation, prompting him to question things he hadn't questioned for years. To think about the boy he'd given up, the sacrifice he'd made because he'd thought it was the right thing.

It might have been, but then you cut him out of your life. How is that being a good father?

It wasn't; that was the issue. What man repudiated his own son?

You never build. You only destroy.

He shoved the thought away and gently, but firmly, put Isla from his lap and back onto the stone seat.

'Orion?'

He didn't look at her, pushing himself off the seat and moving over to the stairs.

'Orion.' There was a splash and when he glanced behind him, she was moving through the water after him. 'I'm sorry. I shouldn't have said anything.' She was upset, he could see that, her golden hair streaming down her back and floating like pretty golden kelp around her white shoulders. Her gaze had darkened. 'Please don't go.'

But the sliver of glass in the centre of his heart, the kernel of ice that had settled there the day he'd left his son for the final time, wouldn't go away. And everything she said only made him more aware of it. More aware of the pain and the rage that he'd thought had been vanquished and hadn't.

He shouldn't be around her when he was like this. It wasn't fair on either of them.

'I have some work to catch up on.' He tried to make his voice sound gentle and yet there was nothing of gentleness in him. 'You can stay here for as long as you like. The northern lights are—'

'I don't care about the northern lights.' The heat of the water had flushed her cheeks a deep pink and with her darkened eyes, she looked like a painting. A Venus in the water. 'I hurt you.'

He laughed because the idea that he'd let anyone hurt him was preposterous. Yet the sound wasn't quite as amused as it should have been. 'You didn't.' He turned away, because if he didn't get out now he was going to ruin her present with his mood and that was unacceptable. 'There are towels—'

Slender arms slid around his waist, holding him tight and a soft, warm body pressed up against his back. He stilled, his heart beating uncomfortably fast.

'Please don't go,' Isla whispered. 'It won't be the same if you're not here.'

It felt as if there was a large boulder sitting on his chest and he wasn't sure why. 'I'm not in the mood for swimming.' His voice was too rough. 'And I don't want to spoil it for you.'

'You won't spoil it for me. I was pushing and I shouldn't have, and I'll stop.'

The tightness in his chest shifted. 'Don't worry. I'll still see you in bed later.'

'I don't… It's not about sex.' Her arms closed tighter around him. 'I want you, your company. Please. Don't let me push you away.'

A cold shock went through him. Is that how she saw it? Did she think this was her fault? Her questions might have touched on some old wounds, but it was his baggage they were dealing with, not hers.

He could have pulled away then. Got out of the pool and headed back to the lodge. Left her there in the night to experience the beauty of the aurora on her own. But she didn't want that, he could hear the plea in her voice.

For some inexplicable reason, a completely baffling reason, she wanted him. And not just his body and the physical pleasure it could bring her, but she wanted *him*. She wanted his company. He couldn't remember the last time someone had wanted that.

His life was all about business, about the hunt. He had colleagues, but he didn't cultivate friends. No one wanted to be friends with a pirate after all, and the ones who did were pirates themselves and he didn't trust them.

The women he slept with loved spending time with him, but only in bed. They didn't want to spend time with *him*. Then again, he'd never encouraged closeness, not with anyone.

He hadn't encouraged it with Isla either and yet somehow, here she was with her arms around him, wanting him to stay. Wanting his company.

Leaving was what he should do. But for some reason, around her, he never did what he should.

Orion turned and looked down. She still had her arms around him, her dark gaze staring up into his, and he knew in that moment he couldn't say no and he couldn't leave. His temper still raged and his heart still ached, and yet when she said 'please' like that and 'it won't be the same without you', he couldn't refuse. He didn't want to refuse. None of this was her fault after all.

'It's not you,' he said quietly. 'You didn't push me away. This is an old wound and your questions brought up some…issues that I thought I'd dealt with. But they're my issues, Isla, not yours. You have nothing to apologise for.'

'Whether they are or not, I'm still sorry. I just don't want you to go.'

He reached down and touched her cheek. 'I don't want to ruin your present.'

'You're not ruining anything.' She leaned into his touch the way she had that morning in bed. 'Please, come and tell me about the aurora.'

The tightness in his chest eased. And he realised that there was nothing he wanted to do more than hold her in the water, in the warmth, watching that sky.

So he put away his pain and his rage, and he held her in his arms the aurora borealis lit up the night sky and turned everything to glory.

CHAPTER TEN

THE NEXT FEW DAYS were amongst the happiest Isla had ever had. She put aside her worries about the company and the board. About David. About her and Orion's marriage. She put aside her worries about the future, full stop. It was the now that mattered and she'd decided to give herself to it wholeheartedly.

They continued the theme of gifts on the twelve days of Christmas and all Orion's gifts were magical. There was another flight to one of Iceland's gorgeous beaches and she saw blue-green icebergs sitting on the black sand like jewels. She took far too many photos of the icebergs and Orion and then made him take some photos of her.

There was an overnight trip to Amsterdam where they went to the Van Gogh Museum and she stayed there for hours, looking at the paintings with Orion patiently at her side. He didn't seem to mind as she waxed lyrical about each painting in great detail, or as he carried the umpteen dozen bags from her raid on the gift shop afterwards. Though that night in the luxury hotel in the middle of town, she made it up to him by letting him do whatever he wanted with her naked body before doing the same for him.

He gave her so many wonderful things and she couldn't help feeling that she was failing by comparison. Her gifts to him were telling him more about her favourite artists and then her favourite foods. She told him about her silly fears and wildest dreams, and how she wished she had more memories of her mother.

She wished she had more to give him than these silly little pieces of herself, but she didn't know what. He didn't seem to need anything else.

Except that scene in the gorge in the hot pool wouldn't stop replaying in her head. Him telling her about the son he'd had taken from him, and then given up. There had been so much anger in his eyes, though he'd tried to dismiss it, and she hadn't made things any easier by pushing him on it.

She should have let it go, but the unfairness of the whole situation made her so angry. He didn't need her anger—it was clear he already had enough of his own—yet she hadn't been able to help it. She could see how it was hurting him and that felt like pain in her own heart too.

She'd only wanted to know why he hadn't contacted his son since, why he'd pretended that Luke didn't exist. The boy would be an adult now and surely if Orion wanted some contact, he could have reached out. He was a man who took what he wanted after all.

Yet he hadn't. And the only reason that made any sense to Isla was that he was afraid, though she didn't know what he'd be afraid of. He might be a corporate pirate but underneath that detachment and ruthlessness, Orion was a good man. Protective, and whether he knew it or not, kind. He might have used a threat to get her to marry him, yet he'd treated her with nothing but respect since they'd arrived. He'd given her choices. He hadn't forced her into anything.

She could understand that he might feel some trepidation about contacting his son, but to simply pretend that the boy didn't exist? She didn't understand that at all. And she might have dismissed it entirely if she hadn't sensed the pain that lay beneath his anger.

The loss of his son had created a wound inside him and it hadn't healed.

She hated that. He was a lion with a thorn in his paw and she wanted to be his Androcles. She wanted to take it out so he could heal.

As the days passed, she thought more about what she could do for him. She didn't stop to ask herself why his pain mattered to her so much, because she didn't want to delve too deeply into the reasons why. And when the idea of the perfect gift for him occurred to her as they flew back to Iceland from Amsterdam, she felt some trepidation. Because it was going to step over a line. Yet she couldn't get it out of her head.

When they returned to the lodge, she did some research, combing through social media to find what she was looking for. She didn't say anything to Orion—they hadn't spoken of anything personal since that night in the pool and she didn't want to rock the boat. Not when every moment she spent with him only made her want to spend more moments. Longer moments.

They discussed every subject under the sun, and she loved how he wasn't afraid to admit it when he didn't know something and how he always wanted to find out more. He told her a little more about his early life in the foster system and they traded stories with a black humour that most other people wouldn't have understood, but they did.

Sometimes he'd go into his office to handle a couple of work things and when he did, she'd go back to her search. Then a few days after they returned from Amsterdam, she finally found what she was looking for: Cleo's social media. Finding her son's after that was relatively easy.

There were pictures of Luke, a tall, handsome young man with coal-black hair and very familiar amber eyes. He looked so much like Orion that Isla's breath caught. And in a strange twist, she discovered that he was studying fine arts at university, and his social media pages were full of pictures of incredible sculptures he'd carved out of rock, and also of a lovely dark-haired girl who was clearly his girlfriend.

It felt wrong to look at pictures of him, to know more about him than his own father, but Isla couldn't stop herself. Besides, it wasn't as if Luke had been difficult to find. Orion could have looked for him at any time, yet he hadn't.

The next day, Orion unveiled his next present to her—a Christmas tree.

It was a living tree in an enormous pot and it was huge, the top almost brushing the ceiling of the lounge, filling the room with the crisp scent of pine. It had been decorated with tinsel and silver baubles and there was an angel on the top.

Isla loved it.

'You told me you'd never had a proper Christmas tree,' Orion said, watching her as she stared up in wonder at the tree. 'So I thought I'd provide you with your first.'

Her heart felt like he'd filled it up with light and now it was pressing painfully against her ribs. A sweet pain. She hadn't thought he'd remember what she'd told him, but he had.

There were even a few carefully wrapped presents under the tree.

'This is amazing,' she said, reaching out to touch one of the delicate blue glass baubles. 'I actually did have a tree once. It was in that family that in the end didn't want me. They put up a little tree and there were decorations on it that their son had made and…and they put up one I had made too.' Her throat closed at the memory. 'It was the first time I felt like I was part of a family.'

There was warmth at her back and then Orion's arms slid around her, pulling her up against the hard heat of his body. 'I know it's not the same,' he murmured. 'But we can have a tree at least.'

Yet it was almost the same. She felt at peace here with him and if she squinted a little, she could imagine that the decorations on the tree had been made by their own children. And a sudden vision filled her head, of Christmas morning here, with the tree up and the fire going, and children unwrapping presents to the sounds of laughter and shrieks of delight.

Her heart clenched tightly in her chest, a shaft of longing piercing her.

She wanted that for herself.

What if this marriage was real? What if it was for ever?

That shaft of longing ached and ached, but she ignored it. Wanting their sham marriage to be real was ridiculous. And she hadn't known him long enough to start entertaining thoughts of a family with him, and apart from anything else, he'd basically implied that he wasn't looking to make a family with anyone. And why would he? When the one he'd had had caused him so much pain?

Which reminded her…

Are you sure this is a good idea?

Isla ignored that thought too. It was an opportunity, that's all it was, and he liked opportunities. He also didn't have to take it if he didn't want it, that was up to him. But he should still have the choice. He should know that there *was* a choice.

She stepped out of his arms and turned. 'I love it, Orion,' she said honestly. 'It's a beautiful gift.'

He smiled, his eyes full of warmth, and her heart caught. He was so gorgeous she sometimes didn't know what to do with herself. 'I hoped you'd like it,' he said. 'Now I'm feeling very smug.'

She wanted to tease him, tell him smugness wasn't a new feeling for him, but she was suddenly nervous. Perhaps this wasn't the right thing to do. But then… She hated the thought of this lion of a man going through the rest of his life with that thorn in his paw. With the constant nagging pain that wouldn't go away.

It wasn't fair. It wasn't right.

She swallowed and reached into her pocket for the piece of paper she'd put there that morning. 'Now it's time for my gift to you,' she said, her heart beating uncomfortably fast in her chest.

Orion frowned slightly. 'You look nervous,' he observed. 'Is it dangerous? An explosive of some kind?'

He was teasing her, which somehow made it worse. Perhaps this would ruin everything. He'd been upset before when she'd tried to push him in the pool about Luke, but… She had to do this. It was an opportunity, that's all.

Isla pulled the piece of paper out of her pocket and held it out. 'No. None of the above.'

Still frowning, Orion took the piece of paper and unfolded it, looking down at what she'd written. His frown deepened. 'What's this?'

Isla shoved her hands into the pockets of her jeans. 'It's an email address.'

'Whose email address?'

She took a breath and met his gaze. 'It's Luke's. Your son's.'

Orion went still, as if he'd been turned to stone, and yet something hot blazed suddenly in his gaze. 'Where did you get it?' He sounded so cool and calm, except she knew he was not. It was that blaze of gold in his eyes that gave it away.

You made a mistake.

A thread of ice wound through her, but she didn't look away. Perhaps this *was* a mistake, yet she'd made it now. There was no other option but to keep going.

'I found Cleo's social media profiles.' She tried to sound as calm as he did. 'And from there it was easy to find Luke's. He's studying fine arts at university, and he has a girlfriend. His email address is there and I thought…' She trailed off, her mouth dry.

Orion was standing so still, yet his golden eyes were blazing bright, fury rolling off him in waves. 'You thought what?' He sounded casual, as if he was asking her whether she preferred tea or coffee.

'I thought you might want to contact him,' she

went on, because she'd given him the piece of paper now and there was no taking it back.

'And what makes you think I might want to do that?' His voice was dangerously soft.

Isla took a breath, her hands clenching in the pockets of her jeans. 'It's an opportunity, Orion. That's all it is. You don't have to take it if you don't want to. But I… I wanted to give it to you nonetheless.'

'Thank you,' Orion said. 'But this is one opportunity I think I'll pass on.' Then he moved over to the fire and casually threw the piece of paper into the flames, before turning around and walking straight out.

Anger moved in his blood like lava and once he was in his office with the door shut behind him, he had to stand in the middle of the room and take a couple of deep breaths just to stop himself from punching his fist through the nearest wall.

How dare she do that to him? How dare she bring up the subject of Luke again, after she'd told him that night in the gorge that she wouldn't? How dare she look for him and find him and *know* him?

It was none of her goddamn business.

'He's doing fine arts at university and he has a girlfriend.'

Orion stormed over to his desk and put his hands flat onto the desktop and leaned on them, staring down at the wood. He couldn't get a breath, rage and pain strangling him.

He didn't want to know. He'd cut Luke out of his life on purpose, because it was easier. Who the hell did she think she was bringing him back again?

'Easier for who? For him or for you?'

She'd said that to him the night in the pool, pushing him, bringing up old doubts and old fears and old agonies. Old griefs he didn't want to deal with and didn't want to face. He wanted them to stay dead and buried where he'd put them.

Behind him he heard a sound, the door opening and slamming shut.

He pushed himself away from the desk and turned around sharply.

Isla had followed him, and stood there in the middle of his office, her golden hair in a cloud around her head, her blue eyes full of sympathy and yet also full of determination. 'I know you're angry with me,' she said. 'And I know I overstepped. I'm sorry. But you have to know that I did it for you. Because you're hurting.'

He bared his teeth at her, struggling to leash the anger that burned inside him. 'Perhaps I wouldn't be if you didn't keep bringing up things I didn't ask you to bring up.'

She didn't seem to be cowed by his anger. She even took a step closer, as if it didn't bother her in the slightest. 'I know that. And you don't have to do anything with the information. The choice is yours.

But… Orion… He deserves to know you.' She took another step closer. 'He deserves to know what kind of father he has.'

Orion felt frozen even as the rage burned inside him. A fruitless, frustrated rage at the past. At all the chances that were taken from him. At the future he wanted so badly that had been denied him. He hadn't thought he'd still feel that, but he did. And it was pointless. The past was dead and gone, and he'd already chosen his future.

'The father he has is a man who destroys things,' he said through gritted teeth. 'A man who takes things apart. He doesn't build anything. He doesn't create. He ruins everything he touches.'

Isla's eyes widened and a terrible compassion crossed her face. She moved, closing the distance between them. 'No,' she said softly, reaching for him 'No, that's not true.'

But before her hands could make contact, he grabbed her wrists, her skin warm against his fingers. He didn't want her to touch him. He couldn't bear the thought of it.

'It is true,' he said harshly, releasing her as quickly as he'd grabbed her. 'I ruined the wedding you planned. I ruined your hope for a family by paying off your fiancé. I threatened you with the destruction of your company to get you to marry me, and I'm still planning on taking it apart when the year is up. Tell me, Isla. What *haven't* I ruined?'

She blinked and he could see the sparkle of tears

in her eyes. It tore something inside him. 'You didn't ruin *anything*,' she said passionately. 'Yes, you did those things, but you didn't force me into anything, Orion. You gave me choices and I made them. And you don't destroy things. You promised to keep the company intact and signed a legal agreement to do so. You created the most lovely Christmas here in the lodge, with a tree and presents. And you made me feel good about myself in a way no one ever has. You made me feel fascinating and precious and beautiful, as if I was worth something.' Her voice thickened, becoming husky. 'You made me feel wanted, Orion. And no one has ever made me feel that way, not one person.'

His chest tightened, but he shoved the feeling away. There was no room for anything but anger in his heart. 'Don't turn this into something it isn't, Isla,' he snapped harshly. 'I *bought* you, remember? Your father sold you to me for the price of Kendricks'. And I only wanted you because I was fascinated by you. It was about *my* fascination, not you.'

She went pale. 'So what are you saying? That everything we shared, everything we talked about, all those things you said to me… You didn't mean any of them? You were only pretending?'

He'd known that would hurt her, yet there wasn't any other way to make her see the truth of what he was. What he'd always been, even as a kid. Intense, desperate, wanting things he could never have. And what he couldn't have, he destroyed, like the bond he'd destroyed with his son. Cutting Luke out of his life as if he didn't exist.

He was selfish, that's what he was, and she needed to understand that.

'Of course, I was only pretending.' He had to force out the words, the rough edge in his voice turning them sharp and jagged. 'Did you truly think I meant any of it?'

She went white, her blue gaze darkening with hurt. 'But…you told me you never said anything you didn't mean.'

He had to end this. He had to bring this whole farce of a honeymoon to an end. He'd call a helicopter for her, send her back to the UK, get her out of his sight and out of his life, and then maybe once she was gone, everything would go back to normal.

'Well,' he said coldly. 'I lied.' He turned and went around the side of his desk, reaching into his pocket for his phone. He kept his gaze on the windows and the landscape outside. It was snowing, which wasn't ideal. 'I'm bringing this to a close, Isla,' he went on. 'It's been a nice week, but I believe I've come to the end of my fascination with you after all. It's time for you to go home.'

There was silence behind him, but he didn't turn around and he wondered if she'd leave him alone now, and felt something else tear inside him at the thought.

But he should have known she wouldn't go quietly. She had fire in her heart, the way he did, and abruptly she was coming around the desk and standing in front of him, small and curvy and as full of anger as he was.

'So you're just going to get rid of me like you did with Luke?' she demanded, apparently not caring that perhaps speaking his son's name wasn't a good idea. 'You're going to cut me out of your life? Pretend I don't exist either?' Hurt glittered in her blue eyes. 'What was it? Was it because I pushed? Because I got angry? Because I wanted too much?'

He held himself rigid, fought the need to reach for her and soothe her pain since that wouldn't make this any easier, not for him or for her. 'It's not you, Isla.'

'I don't believe that,' she flung back, her voice hoarse with pain. 'Not for a second. It's always me, Orion. Always. And no one ever tells me what I'm doing wrong, but it has to be something, otherwise why else would I always be the one who gets sent away?' A tear slid down the side of her nose. 'Why else would I always be the one no one wants?'

He'd wanted to push her away, to get her to storm out and away from him, but the pain in her eyes… Abruptly he hated himself and the lies he'd told her more than he'd thought possible.

He dropped his phone and reached for her, putting his hands on her hips and propelling her back against the windows and pinning her there with his body. She felt warm and soft against him and his rage began to change, to morph into something else, hotter and deeper and more demanding.

'It's nothing *you* did,' he said fiercely, staring down at her, wanting her to believe this if nothing else. 'I'm the destructive one. It's better if you're not anywhere near me.'

She was looking up at him, searching his gaze as if trying to find the truth there. 'I told you, you're not destructive,' she said huskily, somehow bypassing his rage and seeing the agony that still lived in his heart, the grief for the son he'd had to let go. 'Look, I know this is about Luke and I know you're afraid. But both of us understand what it's like to not have our parents in our lives. Wouldn't you want the chance to talk to your dad if you could? Wouldn't you want the chance to know him?'

She's right.

He couldn't remember his father or his mother, and part of him had been glad that he had no memories of them. Who'd want to remember parents who'd put an addiction to a drug over the needs of their own child? At least he hadn't put his son through that.

'Why would Luke want a father like me?' he heard himself say in a voice that didn't sound like his, so hoarse and raw. 'A father who gave him up?'

Isla lifted her hands to his face, her fingers cool on his hot skin. 'You didn't give him up, Orion,' she said softly. 'You gave him happiness. You gave him a place where he was safe and loved, and that's all a child really wants.' Her eyes were full of tears. 'And I know because that's all I ever wanted too.'

He wasn't sure when it changed, when the rage

and the pain turned into heat and desperation. But it did. Perhaps it was the understanding in her eyes, the worry and the hurt that he knew was for him, and how she'd managed to tell him the one thing that made a difference. That walking away from his son had been the right thing to do. And of course she would know, she out of anyone would.

And you hurt her. You hurt her badly.

He'd only wanted to make this easier on both of them. A quick, clean ending. Yet by acting as though none of this past week had meant anything to him, that he'd been pretending all this time, he had hurt her in a place where she was exquisitely vulnerable: her own past and the rejections in it. It had been unconscionable of him and he regretted it with every part of him.

So he kissed her hard and deep, tasting her tears. Tasting her sweetness and the fire inside her. Tasting the understanding he'd never had from any other person. Wanting to give something back to her to make up for his cruelty, his selfishness. Especially when she was right. He'd been wrong to cut Luke out of his life. Wrong to let it go on so long, to pretend that his son didn't even exist. Because he couldn't. He'd never been able to.

'I loved him,' he whispered against her mouth. 'I loved him so much and it killed me to walk away from him.'

'I know.' Her hands were in his hair, smoothing it back. 'And Luke needs to know that too. He needs to know his father cared. You can't deny him, Orion. You can pretend he doesn't exist, but no matter what you do, you'll always be his father. No one can take *that* away from you.'

The truth of it settled down in him like a weight. She was right about that too. It didn't matter how much distance he put between himself and Luke, no matter how much he pretended he didn't have a son, that didn't change the fact that he did. And while life and circumstances had taken away his boy, the fact that he was Luke's father didn't change.

No one could take that away from him.

Need flooded through him, for her and for the gift she'd given him. Because she had given him a gift. The acknowledgement of his son. That he was Luke's father, that his blood ran in Luke's veins and that couldn't be ripped from him. That he was as much a part of his son as his son was part of him.

Orion deepened the kiss, sweeping his tongue inside her mouth, wanting to give her back something as precious as what she'd just given him. Except he didn't have anything except himself and his hunger and that's what he gave her.

Her arms went around his neck and when he picked her up and held her against the glass, she twined her legs around his waist, arching into him. Pressing the soft heat between her thighs against his achingly hard groin, raising her desire to fever pitch.

Orion forgot everything. Everything but the need to be inside her. He held her pinned to the glass as he undid the zip of her jeans, tugging them down and her knickers too until she was open to him. Then he got his own jeans undone and after adjusting their positions slightly, seconds later he was pushing inside her, making them both gasp aloud.

Her blue eyes were dark with desire and he couldn't look away, transfixed by all that burning sapphire. And as he moved inside her, he was conscious of something unfurling inside him, an awareness. Of her. Of the tight wet heat of her sex gripping him. Of her arms around his neck. Of her soft gasps of pleasure. Of her intoxicating scent.

Of her heart of fire.

And he knew.

He'd never get to the bottom of his fascination with her. There would be no end. She would continue to occupy his thoughts for the next week, the next month, the next year. She would continue to occupy his thoughts for ever.

Because his heart burned too and it always had. It burned with love for his son, a love he'd been trying to deny and yet in the end, hadn't been able to. It was too powerful. And now it burned with love for her too.

She'd set it alight that day in the gallery and that fire had never gone out; he just hadn't recognised it. Until now.

He moved harder, deeper, wanting to cover himself with her, inhale her sweetness and take it inside himself, because he knew too how this was going to end. He was going to have to give her up the way he'd given up Luke.

She wanted things he couldn't give her. Things he was done with. She wanted a family and he didn't. He'd had a family and it was gone, and he wasn't going to do it again.

It would hurt her. It would hurt her badly, and yet there was no other way this could go. But before that moment, he could at least give her some pleasure to take with her, so he did, slipping his fingers between her thighs and stroking her as moved. Making her moan and cry out and twist against him.

The orgasm came before he was ready and he wanted to resist it, to draw out the ecstasy for as long as possible, but it was too intense. It swept over both of them, relentless as a king tide, leaving them both gasping, and he held her for a long time against the glass, neither of them speaking.

Finally, he eased away and let her down gently so she was standing once again, then dealt with their clothing, taking his time because this was the last time he would touch her. The last time he'd kiss her, stroke her hair, touch her skin.

It was agony when he finally stepped away, but he did it.

Perhaps she had a sense of what was coming because her face was pale once again, all the pretty colour from her orgasm leached away from her skin. 'You're still going to send me away, aren't you?'

His heart ached at the hurt in her eyes. He hadn't

thought she'd feel so strongly about all of this and that had been careless of him. He should have kept her at a distance. He should have made it all about sex and nothing more. He shouldn't have let her in.

But he had and now there was no help for it. He'd made his choice.

'I'm sorry, Isla.' He had to work to keep the rough edge from his voice. 'But yes, it's time for our honeymoon to end.'

She just stood there staring at him as if he'd made the ground she walked on suddenly disappear under her feet. 'Why? I thought it wasn't me?'

It hurt to look at the bewilderment on her face, but what could he say? Telling her how he felt would only make this even worse for her. Because how could he explain why love was always sacrifice? Why love was always pain? Better to spare her that while he could. She'd have plenty of time to figure that out for herself.

'It's not,' he said. 'But I never wanted a wife, Isla. I never wanted a family. I had one and then I lost it and I'm not doing it again.'

'So it's a choice,' Isla said flatly and it wasn't a question. 'This is something you're actively choosing.'

He didn't understand what she was getting at. 'Yes, didn't I just say that?'

'And what about for someone you loved? Would you do it for them?'

The question caught him off guard and for a second all he could do was stare at her, while his heart shouted, *Yes, I'd do it for you. I love you. And the family you want, I want too, and we could have one together.*

But he swallowed down the words. Because somewhere, somehow, at some point in time, he would destroy that family. He would ruin it, because that's what he did. Or maybe something else would happen and it would be ripped from him once again anyway. Either way, he couldn't risk it happening again. The first time it had just about destroyed him. The next time it would kill him.

'No,' he said quietly. 'Not even then.'

She didn't say anything for the longest time. Then finally all the fight seemed to drain right out of her, and she turned and left his office without a word.

CHAPTER ELEVEN

ISLA DIDN'T KNOW what to do. He'd told her it wasn't her, yet he was sending her away all the same and it didn't make any sense. The way it felt as if he'd ripped her heart out of her chest didn't make any sense either.

She'd only known him a week. What did it matter if he didn't want a family? She'd had that brief, wonderful vision of being here at Christmas time with a family of her own, one with children. Orion's children. And while that vision had made her long for it deeply, she could have that wonderful family Christmas with another man, couldn't she? It didn't have to be with Orion.

She didn't understand why that thought left her so desolate.

He spent the rest of the day in his office, only coming out to tell her that due to the weather, the helicopter wouldn't be able to take her back to the UK until tomorrow.

Getting rid of you the way that family got rid of you. Like David got rid of you.

She couldn't stop thinking about that, or about how Orion had told her that David had sold her to him. Because he had. She hadn't really taken it in when Orion had arrived at the church that day and told her about the deal he'd done with David, because she'd had too many other things to worry about.

But she was thinking about it now. How her happiness or what she wanted had never mattered to him. He hadn't considered those things at all; only the company had ever been important. Never her.

And it was clear she wasn't important to Orion either, if he could get rid of her the way everyone else had, with absolutely no difficulty whatsoever.

It hurt. It hurt so much.

That night he didn't join her in bed the way he normally did, so she lay awake, tossing and turning and aching. Until eventually, sometime before midnight, she got up and went downstairs.

The Christmas tree glowed in the room, the lights turned on and twinkling in the dimness.

She went over to it and sat down, staring up at the lights, her throat feeling sore and her eyes dry and gritty, her thoughts returning to Orion and the desolation she felt at being sent away. The agony seemed disproportionate to what was simply the end of a perfectly lovely affair and she had no idea why.

The end of that scene in his office earlier had been so painful, especially because she'd thought she was getting through to him. She shouldn't have followed him in there after he'd burned the gift of Luke's email address, but she couldn't stand leaving him alone with such pain. She'd wanted him to know that he didn't need to be afraid, that Luke would love him because—

Because you *love him. That's why it hurts so much. That's why you feel so desolate.*

The lights in the tree blurred, the whole world falling away.

She couldn't breathe. Was that true? Had she fallen in love with Orion? Was this why him sending her away left her feeling as though her heart had been ripped out? Why the thought of his pain made her hurt too? And why all she'd been able to see when he'd shown her the Christmas tree, had been children? Their children?

Her eyes closed and it felt as if the weight of an entire mountain was sitting on her chest.

He didn't want a family; he'd been very clear, and it was only now that she understood why. He must have felt this way, standing in the hallway of that house, watching his son. He must have felt this same tearing pain, and it was pain. The pain of wanting something with your whole heart and having to give it up.

No wonder he didn't want to revisit this feeling again. She'd asked him that in his office, if he'd change his mind about having a family with someone he loved, and he'd said no. Yet she hadn't understood the reality of her own question. She understood now, though. She understood completely.

Isla stared up at the lights, feeling tears slide slowly down her cheeks, her heart in agony, not knowing what to do.

You do *know what to do. You know deep down inside.*

Her throat closed. He didn't want her, the way that family hadn't wanted her. The way David didn't want her. Oh, they all thought they did. They'd all liked the idea of her, but when it came to the reality of her in their lives, they'd changed their minds.

And you let them. You never fight to stay.

It was true. That family that sent her back, she'd never told them not to. She'd never told them she wanted to stay. She'd never done that with David either. She'd done what he wanted, because she hadn't felt as if she could rock the boat.

You have so much fight, but you never fight for what you actually want.

A shiver went through her. It was true, she hadn't, and she hadn't because she was afraid. Afraid that even fighting wouldn't be enough. That *she* wouldn't be enough. Just like she hadn't been enough for David or that family. Or Orion.

So, what? You're just going to leave? Like a good little dog?

Isla closed her eyes, her throat aching. But what else could she do? She could fight for what she wanted, fight for more, fight for this marriage they'd entered into, but Orion didn't want that. He'd been very clear. And who was she to change his mind?

He sacrificed having his son in his life in order to make Luke happy. But does that mean he has to sacrifice his own happiness too? Doesn't he deserve some himself? A chance for it at least?

A shiver went through her like a small electric shock. Yes, he *did* deserve more. He deserved a *lot* more. He'd sacrificed everything for his son, leaving precious little for himself except a view of himself as selfish and destructive, which was the opposite of the man he truly was. The man she'd fallen utterly and completely in love with.

That man deserved happiness. That man deserved everything.

And you think you're the one to give it to him? After he told you he didn't want you?

She didn't have much to recommend her. She had a temper and she cared too much about things. She was too stubborn and she pushed when she shouldn't. She wasn't CEO material at all, and she clearly hadn't been daughter material for anyone.

But as he'd shown her, that temper, that passion was a strength, not a weakness. It came from love and he needed to know that. He needed to know that she loved him, that his happiness mattered to her and she was prepared to fight for it.

Her last gift to him would be her heart, and while it might still not be enough for him, it was worth the risk to offer it. Because he was more important than her own fear. Because he was worth it, full stop.

She wiped her eyes and finally got to her feet, and then she turned around.

To find Orion standing behind her, tall and gorgeous and dressed only in a pair of jeans.

She hurriedly wiped her eyes again. 'Sorry. Was I making a noise?'

He stared down at her, his beautiful face enigmatic. 'No. What are you doing up?'

'I couldn't sleep.' She swallowed and straightened. 'I... I've been thinking.'

'Isla—'

'No, let me finish.' She took a breath and squared her shoulders. 'I never fought when that family sent me away. I never told them I wanted to stay. And I never told David that I wanted to be his daughter either. I just did what I was told, because I thought not making a fuss, not rocking the boat, would make me more acceptable. But it didn't.' She swallowed and met his gaze head-on. 'And now I'm tired of not making a fuss. I'm tired of trying to be more acceptable. I'm tired of letting myself be sent away and not fighting for what I want. And what I want is you, Orion. What I want is your happiness. You think you're this terrible, selfish destructive person, but you're not. You think your happiness isn't important, but it is. It is to me.' She gripped tight to her courage and looked into his dark amber gaze, letting her conviction burn in hers. 'I know you don't want a family again. I know you don't want a wife. But you loved your son so much, and I think that no matter what you tell yourself, you *do* want that. And I can give it to you. I *want* to give it to you.'

She glanced at the clock on the mantelpiece and saw that it had just turned twelve, so she glanced back. 'So today's gift to you is my heart, Orion. Because I love you.'

Orion didn't understand the words at first. He'd got up because he hadn't been able to sleep either, and had seen her sitting under the tree. There had been tears on her cheeks and his heart had twisted and ached. He shouldn't have gone to her. He'd made the right decision yesterday to give her up, for her own good, and he thought he wouldn't regret that decision.

Yet all he felt was regret. Especially now, because apparently, she loved him and he had no idea, no idea at all what to do with that. It didn't make any sense after yesterday, when he'd been so cruel to her.

'Why?' he said, unable to think of a single reason why she should.

'Because you're kind and patient, and caring and strong. Because you took me to Amsterdam and listened to me witter on about Van Gogh, and asked me questions and were interested. And you took me to a volcano and you showed me how to skate, and you showed me the northern lights.' She took a step forward, her blue gaze fierce. 'You showed me pleasure and you showed me your pain. You showed me your heart and you showed me your love. And I... I will never be the same, Orion. How could I? I didn't know what love was until you told me about Luke and what you did for him, and then I couldn't understand how he wouldn't love you. Because I loved you.' She took another step. 'All I want is happiness for you—I don't care about anything else. So please let me try. Please let me try to make you happy.'

She was so beautiful standing under the tree, her dark blue eyes glittering like the lights of the tree itself. Like the aurora.

The gift of her heart. She had already given him so much, how could he say no? He loved her already and what she was offering him...he wanted it so badly. He *wanted* it.

She deserves happiness, too, and hers is just as important as yours.

He didn't want another family. He couldn't bear the thought. But he also couldn't bear the thought of her giving up her own happiness for him. He didn't want her doing what he'd done all those years ago, sacrificing a future for love.

So give it to her. You want it too. Don't deny it.

'You shouldn't love me, Isla,' he heard himself say. 'All I'll do is hurt you.'

She lifted a shoulder, seeming casual, yet there were more tears in her eyes. 'It's too late for that, I love you already.'

You want this. You want more. You want it all. You always have.

He did—he could feel it, burning there in his heart. A bone-deep longing for love, family, a home, a place where he belonged. For children that were his, that he didn't have to give up and a woman at his side whom he loved and who loved him. No more breaking. No more destroying. Only building. Only creating.

You can't send her away. You can't reject her like everyone else. She deserves more than that.

He felt as if he was on the edge of a cliff and the wild wind was trying to pull him off. 'Isla...' He couldn't sound detached now and he didn't even try. 'If you were smart, you'd leave me. You'd get on that helicopter and you'd never come back.'

There was something hot in her blue eyes, something fierce. The love she'd offered him, her burning heart. 'Do you want me to? Do you really want me to?'

He should have said yes. He should have turned and walked away. But he couldn't, not this time. The thought of her pain if he sent her away was too much, because no, she *didn't* deserve that. She didn't deserve to bear the brunt of his fear. And that's what it was, wasn't it? Fear of the pain that love was, fear of risking his heart again. Fear that he didn't deserve this second chance somehow.

But she thought he did, and she thought his happiness was important, and what was important to her, was also important to him, so...how could he refuse her? How could he let his pain and fear be more important than her love? He couldn't.

Something burst free in him in that moment and it came to him, in a sudden rush of insight, that loving her wasn't a sacrifice. Loving her didn't mean having to give her up. Loving her meant joy. Loving her meant happiness, because that's what he'd had with her here in this little lodge.

For the first time in his life, he'd been happy. And he could keep that happiness if he wanted it. He could keep it for ever.

Orion North was a man who took what he wanted and so he took what she offered him. Because he wanted it more than he wanted his next breath.

'No,' he said roughly. 'No, I don't.' And somehow the distance between them was gone and she was in his arms, warm and soft against him, her face pressed to his chest.

'I want this,' she said, her voice muffled. 'I want you. I want everything, Orion. If you truly don't want a family, that's okay. We don't have to have one. I can—'

He took her face between his palms and kissed her before she could go on, and then he lifted his mouth and looked down into her eyes. And he let the wind pull him off the cliff and he was flying. 'No,' he said. 'I don't want you giving up what you want for me. What you want is important, because *you're* important. I told you the truth yesterday, when I said you weren't a fascination to me any more. You aren't. Because you're more than a fascination, more than an interest.' He bent and brushed his mouth over hers. 'The truth is that I love you. And I have loved you since that moment I saw you in the gallery, luminous and beautiful and everything I ever wanted.'

Something lit in her face then, an incandescence that ignited something in him. 'Can we stay married then? Please. I don't want anyone else to be my husband but you.'

'Yes.' He brushed another kiss over her mouth. 'We'll stay married for a year. For five. For ten. For ever, Snow White, and that's a promise.'

She put her arms around his neck, arching into him. 'We don't have to have many children. Just one if that's all you want.'

He tightened his hold on her, because she was where she'd always been meant to be. Where he'd always wanted her to be right from the first moment he saw her. Here in his arms. 'We will have as many children as you want.'

'And Christmas. I want a proper Christmas.'

'Always. Every Christmas will be a proper one.' Then, because he'd had enough of talking, he covered her mouth and kissed her hard and deep and long.

Orion had always thought love was pain, an agonising sacrifice. He'd never known that love could also be joy, a foundation of happiness on which to build a life.

And together they built that life,
And it was glorious.

EPILOGUE

CHRISTMAS MORNING AT the lodge was always chaos, but Isla didn't mind.

She sat on the couch next to Orion, while their twins, Ava and Molly, squealed with delight as they opened their presents.

Orion had their new son in the crook of his arm, rocking him absently as he talked to Luke, who had joined them for Christmas this year.

It had taken Orion at least a few months to get in contact with Luke, but after Isla had fallen pregnant with the twins, Orion had finally taken that step and emailed him. Isla had been worried, desperately hoping that Luke would in fact want to get in contact and afraid that for all her confidence, he wouldn't.

Yet she needn't have worried. Luke was ecstatic to meet his father and the two had hit it off immediately, getting on like a house on fire. The relationship they'd built together over the past few years had healed the wound in Orion's heart, as had the birth of his children.

It had healed Isla too.

David would never be a father to her, but after she'd returned from Iceland with Orion, she'd realised she didn't want him to be. She had the acceptance and love she'd craved from her husband, and she didn't need it from him or from the board of Kendricks'.

Certainly she didn't need it after Orion bought Kendricks' and Isla became CEO. Orion had decided he was done with corporate raiding and wanted to try growing a company instead of taking it apart, and so he'd become her CFO instead, the two of them deciding to channel much of Kendricks' profits into charitable enterprises. Luke had even offered to design some special Christmas ornaments they could use as fundraising items.

Molly was kneeling in a sea of wrapping paper and demanding Luke's help with building the plastic brick spaceship that he'd given her for Christmas, and when he got off the couch to help her, Isla glanced up at her husband. Only to find him looking back, his wolf-gold eyes gleaming.

'You look happy, Snow White,' he said, the special smile he saved just for her playing around his mouth.

'Yes,' she said simply. 'I'm the happiest I've ever been.'

Orion's smile deepened into something so hot it could have melted all the ice in Iceland. 'That sounds like a challenge to me.'

Then he set about proving that, while she might

be the happiest she'd ever been in that moment, there could be moments when she was even happier.

And as it turned out he was right.

* * * * *

If you got lost in the passion of
His Innocent Unwrapped in Iceland
then you're sure to love these other
Jackie Ashenden stories!

Stolen for My Spanish Scandal
The Maid the Greek Married
Wed for Their Royal Heir
Her Vow to Be His Desert Queen
Pregnant with Her Royal Boss's Baby

Available now!

#4161 BOUND BY HER BABY REVELATION
Hot Winter Escapes
by Cathy Williams

Kaya's late mentor was like a second mother to her. So Kaya's astounded to learn she won't inherit her home—her mentor's secret son will. Tycoon Leo plans to sell the property and return to his world. But soon their impalpable desire leaves them forever bound by the consequence...

#4162 AN HEIR MADE IN HAWAII
Hot Winter Escapes
by Emmy Grayson

Nicholas Lassard never planned to be a father. But when business negotiations with Anika Pierce lead to his penthouse, she's left with bombshell news. He vows to give his child the upbringing he never had, but before that, he must admit that their connection runs far deeper than their passion...

#4163 CLAIMED BY THE CROWN PRINCE
Hot Winter Escapes
by Abby Green

Fleeing an arranged marriage to a king is easy for Princess Laia—remaining hidden is harder! When his brother, Crown Prince Dax, tracks her down, she strands them on a private island. Laia's unprepared for their chemistry, and ten days alone in paradise makes it impossible to avoid temptation!

#4164 ONE FORBIDDEN NIGHT IN PARADISE
Hot Winter Escapes
by Louise Fuller

House-sitting an idyllic beachside villa gives Jemima Friday the solitude she craves after a gut-wrenching betrayal. So when she runs into charismatic stranger Chase, their instant heat is a complication she doesn't need! Until they share a night of unrivaled pleasure on his lavish yacht, and it changes *everything*...

#4165 A NINE-MONTH DEAL WITH HER HUSBAND
Hot Winter Escapes
by Joss Wood
Millie Piper's on-paper marriage to CEO Benedikt Jónsson gave her ownership over her life and her billion-dollar inheritance. Now Millie wants a baby, so it's only right that she asks Ben for a divorce first. She doesn't expect her shocking attraction to her convenient husband! Dare she propose that *Ben* father her child?

#4166 SNOWBOUND WITH THE IRRESISTIBLE SICILIAN
Hot Winter Escapes
by Maya Blake
Shy Giada Parker can't believe she agreed to take her überconfident twin's place in securing work with ruthless Alessio Montaldi. Until a blizzard strands her in Alessio's opulent Swiss chalet and steeling her body against his magnetic gaze becomes Giada's hardest challenge yet!

#4167 UNDOING HIS INNOCENT ENEMY
Hot Winter Escapes
by Heidi Rice
Wildlife photographer Cara prizes her independence as the only way to avoid risky emotional entanglements. Until a storm traps her in reclusive billionaire Logan's luxurious lodge, and there's nowhere to hide from their sexual tension! Logan's everything Cara shouldn't want but he's all she craves...

#4168 IN BED WITH HER BILLIONAIRE BODYGUARD
Hot Winter Escapes
by Pippa Roscoe
Visiting an Austrian ski resort is the first step in Hope Harcourt's plan to take back her family's luxury empire. Having the gorgeous security magnate Luca Calvino follow her every move, protecting her from her unscrupulous rivals, isn't! Especially when their forbidden relationship begins to cross a line...

YOU CAN FIND MORE INFORMATION ON UPCOMING HARLEQUIN TITLES, FREE EXCERPTS AND MORE AT HARLEQUIN.COM.

HPCNMRB1123

Get 3 FREE REWARDS!

We'll send you 2 FREE Books plus a FREE Mystery Gift.

FREE Value Over $20

Both the **Harlequin® Desire** and **Harlequin Presents®** series feature compelling novels filled with passion, sensuality and intriguing scandals.

YES! Please send me 2 FREE novels from the Harlequin Desire or Harlequin Presents series and my FREE gift (gift is worth about $10 retail). After receiving them, if I don't wish to receive any more books, I can return the shipping statement marked "cancel." If I don't cancel, I will receive 6 brand-new Harlequin Presents Larger-Print books every month and be billed just $6.30 each in the U.S. or $6.49 each in Canada, a savings of at least 10% off the cover price, or 3 Harlequin Desire books (2-in-1 story editions) every month and be billed just $7.83 each in the U.S. or $8.43 each in Canada, a savings of at least 12% off the cover price. It's quite a bargain! Shipping and handling is just 50¢ per book in the U.S. and $1.25 per book in Canada.* I understand that accepting the 2 free books and gift places me under no obligation to buy anything. I can always return a shipment and cancel at any time by calling the number below. The free books and gift are mine to keep no matter what I decide.

Choose one: ☐ **Harlequin Desire**
(225/326 BPA GRNA)   ☐ **Harlequin Presents Larger-Print**
(176/376 BPA GRNA)   ☐ **Or Try Both!**
(225/326 & 176/376 BPA GRQP)

Name (please print)

Address   Apt. #

City   State/Province   Zip/Postal Code

Email: Please check this box ☐ if you would like to receive newsletters and promotional emails from Harlequin Enterprises ULC and its affiliates. You can unsubscribe anytime.

Mail to the Harlequin Reader Service:
IN U.S.A.: P.O. Box 1341, Buffalo, NY 14240-8531
IN CANADA: P.O. Box 603, Fort Erie, Ontario L2A 5X3

Want to try 2 free books from another series! Call 1-800-873-8635 or visit www.ReaderService.com.

*Terms and prices subject to change without notice. Prices do not include sales taxes, which will be charged (if applicable) based on your state or country of residence. Canadian residents will be charged applicable taxes. Offer not valid in Quebec. This offer is limited to one order per household. Books received may not be as shown. Not valid for current subscribers to the Harlequin Presents or Harlequin Desire series. All orders subject to approval. Credit or debit balances in a customer's account(s) may be offset by any other outstanding balance owed by or to the customer. Please allow 4 to 6 weeks for delivery. Offer available while quantities last.

Your Privacy—Your information is being collected by Harlequin Enterprises ULC, operating as Harlequin Reader Service. For a complete summary of the information we collect, how we use this information and to whom it is disclosed, please visit our privacy notice located at corporate.harlequin.com/privacy-notice. From time to time we may also exchange your personal information with reputable third parties. If you wish to opt out of this sharing of your personal information, please visit readerservice.com/consumerschoice or call 1-800-873-8635. **Notice to California Residents**—Under California law, you have specific rights to control and access your data. For more information on these rights and how to exercise them, visit corporate.harlequin.com/california-privacy.

HDHP23

HARLEQUIN
PLUS

Try the best multimedia subscription service for romance readers like you!

Read, Watch and Play.

Experience the easiest way to get the romance content you crave.

Start your **FREE TRIAL** at
www.harlequinplus.com/freetrial.